D0483752

About the author

Håkan Nesser is one of Sweden's most famous crime writers. He made his name with his popular series featuring Inspector Van Veeteren, authored the highly-acclaimed series focusing on Inspector Gunnar Barbarotti and is also known for a number of exciting stand-alone novels, including *A Summer with Kim Novak*. His award-winning books have been made into TV series and films and enjoy great international success.

About the translator

Saskia Vogel's translations include *All Monsters Must Die: An Excursion to North Korea* by Magnus Bärtås and Fredrik Ekman, *Who Cooked Adam Smith's Dinner?* by Katrine Marçal, and works of fiction by Rut Hillarp and Lina Wolff, among others.

A Summer with Kim Novak

Håkan Nesser

A Summer with Kim Novak

Translated from the Swedish
by Saskia Vogel

World Editions

Published in Great Britain in 2015 by World Editions Ltd., London

www.worldeditions.org

Copyright © Håkan Nesser, 1998
English translation copyright © Saskia Vogel, 2015
Cover design Multitude
Image credit © 123rf.com

First published as *Kim Novak badade aldrig i Genesarets sjö* by Albert
Bonniers Förlag, Stockholm, Sweden 1998. Published in the English
language by arrangement with Bonnier Rights, Stockholm, Sweden.

British Library Cataloguing-in-Publication Data
A catalogue record for this book is available on request from
the British Library

ISBN 978-94-6238-025-7

Typeset in Minion Pro

The cost of this translation was defrayed by a subsidy from
the Swedish Arts Council, gratefully acknowledged

Distribution Europe (except the Netherlands and Belgium):
Turnaround Publisher Services, London
Distribution the Netherlands and Belgium: Centraal Boekhuis,
Culemborg, the Netherlands

In memory of Gunnar

I

1

This story is going to be about the Incident, and of course it will be, but there's so much more to it. That fateful event is why I remember the summer of 1962 more clearly than any other summer of my youth. It cast its dismal pall over so many things. Over me and over Edmund. Over my poor parents, my brother, and that entire time of my life. My memories of that town out on the plain—the people, our experiences and the particular circumstances of our lives—would have been lost to the well of time if it weren't for that grisly act. The Incident.

Where to begin? I could have started anywhere, and eventually I got tired of considering all the possibilities, so I decided to pinpoint an average weekday, at home in my kitchen on Idrottsgatan. Just my father and me, one balmy evening in May.

'It's going to be a difficult summer,' my father said. 'Let's face it.'

He swilled the burnt gravy into the sink and coughed. I looked at his slightly hunched back and pondered. He wasn't usually a Jeremiah, so I suspected that this was serious.

'I can't manage any more,' I said and rolled the under-cooked potatoes to the meat side of the plate, to make it look as though I'd at least eaten half. He came over to the kitchen table and looked at my leftovers for a few seconds. Sadness flickered across his face. He could see right through me, but still he took the plate and scraped the remains into the bucket under the sink without a word.

'Like I said, a difficult summer,' he replied instead, his crooked back turned toward me.

'It is what it is,' I answered.

Those words were his cure-all, and I used them so he could see I wanted to be supportive. To show that we were in this together and that I had indeed learned a thing or two over the years.

'Truer words were never spoken,' he said. 'Man proposes but God disposes.'

'You said it,' I replied.

Because it was a rather fine May evening, I went to Benny's after dinner. As usual, Benny was in the loo so first I had to talk to his miserable mum in the kitchen.

'How's your mother doing?' she asked.

'It's going to be a difficult summer,' I said.

She nodded and took her handkerchief from her apron pocket and blew her nose. Benny's mum suffered from allergies off and on during the summer. They said it was hay fever. When I think back, I think she had 'hay fever' all year round.

'That's what my dad said,' I added.

'Ah yes,' she said. 'Only time will tell.'

Recently, I had begun to understand that this was how adults spoke. It wasn't just my father; this was how you showed that you weren't wet behind the ears. Since my mother had fallen ill and ended up in hospital, I'd noted the most important expressions and used them accordingly.

It is what it is.

Same old, same old.

It could have been worse.

Life is a mystery.

Or why not 'Keep your chin up, and your feet on the ground', as Cross-eyed Karlesson at the corner shop declared a hundred times a day.

Or 'Only time will tell,' à la Mrs. Barkman.

Benny was called Barkman, too. Benny Jesias Conny Barkman. Some people thought it a strange string of names, but I never heard him complain.

We find many names for those we love, his mum would say with a grin that exposed her grey-tinged gums.

And then Benny would tell her to shut her mouth.

Even though I had one foot in the adult world, I couldn't help but wonder why people didn't just keep quiet when they had nothing to say. Like Mrs. Barkman—and Cross-Eyed Karlesson, who sometimes jabbered so incessantly he didn't stop to breathe. It made an awful sound.

When she'd taken the handkerchief away from her nose, Mrs. Barkman asked, 'How's she doing?'

'Same old, same old,' I said and shrugged. 'Not great, I reckon.'

Mrs. Barkman wrung her hands in her lap and her eyes filled with tears, but it was probably just the hay fever. She was a big woman who always wore floral dresses, and my father said she was a touch simple-minded. I had no idea what he meant by that and I didn't really care. I wanted to talk to Benny, not his weepy mum.

'He goes to the loo a lot,' I said, mostly to seem grown-up and to keep the conversation going.

'He has a nervous stomach,' she said. 'He gets it from his dad.'

A nervous stomach? That was the stupidest thing I'd heard all day. A stomach can't be nervous, can it? I guessed she'd said that because of her simple-mindedness, and it wasn't worth pursuing.

'Is she still in hospital?'

I nodded. I didn't see the point in talking to her any more.

'Have you been to visit her?'

I nodded again. Of course I had. What was she on about? It had been a week since my last visit, but it was what it was. The important thing was that my dad went to the hospital nearly every day. Even someone like Mrs. Barkman should know that.

'Well, you know what they say,' she said. 'We all have our crosses to bear.'

She sighed and blew her nose. The toilet flushed and Benny came running out.

'Hi, Erik,' he said. 'I shat like a horse. Let's get out of here and raise hell.'

'Benny,' his mum said wanly. 'Language.'

'Damn it, right,' said Benny.

Nobody swore as much as Benny did. Not on our street. Not in our school. Probably not even in the whole town. When we were in third grade, or maybe fourth, a tetchy teacher with an underbite arrived at school. All the way from Göteborg. They said she had a natural gift for teaching, and her main subject was Religious Education. After hearing Benny curse a blue streak for a few days, she decided to sort him out. She was given permission by the headmaster, Mr. Stigman, and our class teacher Mr. Wermelin to work on Benny's speech twice a week. I think they started in September and carried on throughout the autumn term. Around Christmas Benny developed a stutter so severe that no one could understand him. Come spring, the teacher from Göteborg was fired, Benny started swearing again and by the summer holidays he was back to his old self.

On the May evening that my father said it would be a difficult summer, Benny and I went out to sit inside the culvert. Or rather, we started our evening there. The culvert was a point of departure for whatever the night had in store for us. It lay in a dry ditch fifty metres into the forest, and God knows how it ended up there. It was about one and a half metres in diameter and the same in depth. Because it was tilted on its side, it was a good hideout if you wanted to be left alone. Or needed shelter from the rain. Or were hatching plans and sneaking a few John Silvers that you made some little kid buy for you, so you didn't have to show your face at Karlesson's shop. Or, as a last resort, that you had bought yourself.

On this particular evening we had a couple of cigarettes stashed in a can under a tree-root right beside the culvert. Benny dug them out. We smoked with our usual reverence. Then we discussed what sounded better: ciggies or fags. And the right way to hold a cigarette. Thumb–index finger or index finger–middle finger. We didn't reach a verdict on any of those issues that day either.

Then Benny asked me about my mother.

'Your mum,' he said. 'Shit, is she going to …?'

I nodded.

'Think so,' I said. 'Dad says so. The doctors say so.'

Benny searched his vocabulary.

'That's bloody horrible,' he finally said.

I shrugged. Benny had been close to his aunt, and she had died, so I knew that he knew what he was talking about.

On the other hand, I had no idea what it was like.

Dead?

When I thought about it—and I'd thought about it often this cold, comfortless spring—all I knew was that it was the strangest word in the entire language.

Dead?

Inconceivable. The worst part was that my dad seemed to have as weak a grip on the concept as I did. I could tell by his face the one time—the only time—I asked what it actually meant. What it actually meant to be dead.

'Hmm, well,' he had muttered, still staring at the TV with the sound turned down. 'Only time will tell.'

'A difficult summer,' Benny repeated thoughtfully. 'For Christ's sake, Erik, you'll have to write to me. I'm going to be up in Malmberget until school starts, but if you need any advice, you can count on me.'

There was a sudden lull in our conversation, as if we had been touched by an angel. I felt it as clearly as anything, and I knew that Benny had felt it, too, because he cleared his throat and solemnly repeated his offer.

'Bloody hell, Erik. Write and tell me how you're doing.'

We shared the second and last wrinkled cigarette. I think I did write a letter to Benny; sometime in July, when everything was at its worst, but I can't really remember. What I do know is that I never heard a peep from him.

Benny Barkman wasn't one for pen and paper.

During these years in the early 1960s, my dad worked at the jail. It was a taxing job, especially for someone as sensitive as he was, but he never talked about it. He avoided unpleasant topics, in general.

Sufficient unto the day is the evil thereof, and all that.

He'd arrived in the town on the plain in the 1930s, in the middle of the Depression; met my mother and got her pregnant around the time the world went mad for the second time that century. My brother Henry was born on 1 June 1940; three days later, after taking leave from his post up in Lapland, my father arrived at the bedside of his wife and child, bearing freshly picked lilies of the valley and forty cans of military-issue liver pâté.

So the story goes.

He never went back up north. After his first son was born, he managed to get out of his military service for the rest of the war. He blamed it on his back, I think. He found a job in one of the town's many shoe factories, where the army's winter boots were made. So in a way he was still doing his duty. A few years after the end of the Second World War, the family moved into a flat on Idrottsgatan.

As for me, I was born eight years and eight days after my brother, and I grew up with the feeling that the age difference between us was much greater than between him and our parents. Now, at the start of the sixties, I had begun to see that this was a misconception. Perhaps my mother's cancer had helped clarify matters.

My mother and father were quite old, you see. The summer my mother was about to die, they were both fifty-seven. One hundred and fourteen years between them. A dizzying sum. Henry turned twenty-two in June. I was fourteen. My father had worked in the prison since it opened its doors to the country's most dangerous criminals a year and a half earlier.

Or rather, it shut its doors behind them.

He was a screw; a word that had never been uttered in the town before the Grey Giant appeared out on the plain.

He called himself a prison guard. Everyone else said screw. A screw at the Grey Giant.

Previously, he'd worked as a shoe-binder at a number of factories. The disappearance of the word 'shoe-binder' roughly coincided with the factory shutting down and the arrival of the screws. This was the way of the world, it seemed. One thing disappears, only to be replaced by something else. And that goes for events and all manner of phenomena as well as people.

It seems that the only place where everything stays put is inside your head, but there, too, things go missing.

One factory that didn't shut down during those years was the Jam & Juice where my mother worked. Until she fell ill, that is. Having a father at the shoe factory and a mother at the Juicy had its perks. You always had swish shoes and there was usually a generous supply of apple juice down in the cellar.

But that summer, we were nearing the end of an era. Having a screw for a dad came with no perks at all.

As for my brother Henry, he was expected to continue his studies and then move up a rung or two on the social ladder, but that didn't really go as planned. He did matriculate at the secondary grammar school—a prestigious all-boys school in Örebro that stood opposite a thousand-year-old castle surrounded by a moat. Up to that point, it was looking good. He studied and took the train to the county capital and back every day.

Just after his second semester, Henry ran away. It was the autumn of 1957 and it would be more than a year before he knocked on the door at Idrottsgatan again, carrying a sailor's bag and with a bunch of bananas on his back. He had been around the world, he explained, but had spent most of his time in Hamburg and Rotterdam. He had a rose tattooed on his arm. It was clear to us all that he didn't really want to move up in the world, at least not in the way our parents had hoped. When Henry returned, my mother cried. I'm not sure if it was for joy or out of despair over his tattoo. After taking it easy for a few months, Henry set off again, roving the seven seas until 1960. When he came home the next time, on the same day that Dan Waern failed to win the bronze medal for the 1,500 metres in Rome, he said that he'd had enough of the sea. He started freelancing for *Kurren*, the regional newspaper, and found himself a fiancée. One Emmy Kaskel, who worked at Blidberg's men's outfitters. She had the best breasts in town.

Probably in the whole world.

In just about the same breath he found a flat twenty kilometres from home in Örebro, where *Kurren* also had their headquarters. His bedsit was roughly the size of two ping-pong tables; it didn't have its own toilet or running water, and yet every now and then Emmy Kaskel bared her glorious breasts and more in that tiny flat.

At least that's what Benny and I assumed.

But she didn't move in with him. Emmy was two years younger than Henry and still lived at home with her parents. They were missionaries and had a discount at Blidberg's. My brother said half of the town was involved in the Free Church malarkey, so their affiliation was nothing to worry about.

There's nothing we do out here that they don't do in there, he'd say with a wry smile.

'Look who it is,' my father said when I came home that balmy evening in May.

I could tell he had something on his mind, so I sat down at the kitchen table with last year's apple juice and some biscuits and flipped through an old issue of *Reader's Digest*, which Grandpa Wille gave us a massive stack of for Christmas every year. He was the twelfth best chess player in Sweden and owned a milk bar in Säffle.

'Erik, this is big,' said my father.

'It is what it is,' I answered.

'You're probably going to have to go and stay at Gennesaret this summer.'

'Sure,' I said.

'You'll have a good time. I've had a word with Henry. He and Emmy'll be there as well and they'll take care of you.'

'I'll be fine,' I said.

'I know,' said my father. 'Edmund might join you.'

'Edmund?' I said.

'Why not?' said my father and scratched his neck nervously. 'So you'll have some company your own age.'

'Well,' I said. 'Sufficient unto the day is the evil thereof.'

2

The school was three storeys tall—shaped like a shoebox and built from yellowish Pomeranian stone that had darkened to brown over the years. On one side of the building was a gravel yard used as a football pitch at breaktime. On the other side was another playground where you could have played football, but no one did.

The anti-football crowd kept to this other side, as did the girls, who clustered together, trading things and gossiping. Well, I don't actually know if they traded things, or what they got up to, because I always kept a safe distance.

I belonged to a group of a dozen or so boys who didn't spend their breaktime getting dirty on the football pitch. We were the anti-football crowd. In my heart of hearts, I had to admit that I hated sports, and I had no idea how all the football players fitted on the pitch each break; there must have been at least fifty of them. But perhaps only a score of the best players actually kicked the ball, leaving the others to stand around and shout and get as grimy as possible. I don't know. I never watched them play. I was on the girls' side, as I said. My choice of location wasn't going to impress anyone, but I tried to convince myself that there were more important things in life.

And I wasn't alone. Benny was there, along with Snukke, Balthazar Lindblom, Veikko, Arse-Enok, and a few others.

And Edmund.

After my father had suggested that we might spend the summer together, I realized I didn't actually know anything about him.

I knew what everyone knew: his father read girlie mags, and he was born with six toes on each foot.

Otherwise, he was a blank page. He was tall and hefty. His glasses always seemed to be missing a lens or a side piece. We'd only been in the same class this past year, and there were rumours that he had a great big model train set and a great big collection of Wild West magazines, but I didn't know if either was true.

His father was also a screw; that was the connection. He and my father had been working together for the past year, and that's probably how they had come to discuss their plans for the summer, and one thing must have led to another.

I didn't exactly have any commitments—except perhaps with Benny, who was out of the picture the whole summer anyway—so after circling each other warily over the course of a few breaktimes, I tested the waters.

'Hi, Edmund,' I said.

'Hi,' said Edmund.

We were standing by the bike racks under the corrugated metal roof, casually kicking gravel at the girls' bikes.

'My dad mentioned something,' I said.

'I heard,' said Edmund.

'Oh yeah?' I said.

'Yep,' said Edmund.

Then the bell rang. And that was it for a few days. It was a promising start.

Gennesaret wasn't the name of the lake. It was the name of a house by a lake called Möckeln. It's still called Möckeln, incidentally.

It was twenty-five kilometres from town and it took more than two hours to get there by bike, but only an hour and a half back. The journey times varied because of Kleva, a punishing hill that rose to 1,300 metres about halfway there.

Möckeln—a large, almost circular brown lake—was surrounded by a number of villages, but it was dominated by forest-fringed beaches. Gennesaret sat in solitary splendour on a pine-clad point and was part of my mother's inheritance. A two-storey tumbledown wooden shack with no comforts other than a roof over your head and fresh lake water ten metres away. The ice usually took the jetty out every winter, and there was an outboard motor for the rowing boat that had lain in pieces in a shed since I was born.

My dying mother wasn't the sole owner of this house. There was an Aunt Rigmor who had inherited half of it, but she wasn't of sound mind and therefore couldn't lay claim to it.

Rigmor's tragic condition was the result of an accident that took place during one of the first summers of the war. The story had as firm a place in our family history as the Fall does in the Bible: she had collided with an elk; but what gave the story its mythological air was the fact that she was riding a bicycle at the time. Aunt Rigmor, that is, not the elk. She and a friend had been on a cycling holiday in Småland, and while freewheeling down one of the hills in the uplands she'd charged right into a magnificent twelve-pointer and then straight through the doors of the notorious Dingle asylum on the West Coast.

Never to be discharged, it seemed. I had only seen pictures of her and she didn't resemble Mum in the slightest. She looked more like a seal, actually, but with glasses and no moustache. Fitting for someone in Dingle.

If my tragic aunt hadn't been in the picture in the first place, it's likely that my parents wouldn't have held on to Gennesaret. For some reason, they never seemed to like it out there.

It wasn't cosy. Maybe that was it. Or maybe it was because my mother never learned how to swim. The lake was deep. In parts. Certainly beyond our neck of land.

Whatever the case, that May I had a hard time picturing how the summer would unfold. Or how things would be with Henry and Emmy. I couldn't think about Emmy without picturing her breasts. Covered by clothing, but still. And I couldn't picture her breasts without getting a boner. It was what it was.

The thought of what my brother would get up to with Emmy Kaskel wasn't easy to cope with either. Gennesaret wasn't a big house.

And on top of all that, there was Edmund. I had no idea how things would play out.

But sod it, I thought. Only time will tell.

Ewa Kaludis began work at Stava School on a Thursday. We'd just had double woodwork and I'd comprehensively ruined the magazine rack I'd been working on for the past seven months. Our carpentry teacher Gustav wasn't happy about it, but it felt good. Whether it was sewing or woodwork, I didn't like arts and crafts; they never turned out quite the way you thought they would, and they always took bloody ages.

As usual, I was hanging out around the bike shed together

with Benny and Arse-Enok, waiting for the end of break, when she appeared on the street.

I'd like to say that I saw her first, but both Benny and Arse-Enok are equally sure that they did. It doesn't really matter; the point is that she arrived. I realized she must have passed the football pitch first, because within a few seconds the girls' side was chock-a-block with people gawking. Swarms of filthy football players.

'Bloody hell,' said Benny. His mouth was so wide open that it looked as if he was at the dentist waiting for Dr. Slaktarsson to start drilling.

'It's Kim Novak,' said Arse-Enok.

As for me, I said nothing. Under normal circumstances, I wasn't one to comment for the sake of it, but at this moment I was dumbstruck. It was like in a film. But better. The woman who came roaring in on her moped really did look like Kim Novak. Big wheat-blond hair, tied back with a foxy red hair-band. Dark, foxy sunglasses and a full, foxy mouth that made me weak in the knees. She wore slim black slacks, a thin black top that hugged her breasts and a red-and-black-checked Swanson shirt, unbuttoned and billowing in the wind.

'Holy bloody hell, what a fox,' said Balthazar Lindblom.

'It's a Puch,' said Arse-Enok. 'Bloody hell, Kim Novak is rolling in to our schoolyard on a Puch. *Kiss me, stupid.*'

With that, Arse-Enok fainted. He suffered from some sort of mild epilepsy that knocked him out on occasion. It came as no surprise that this proved to be too much for him.

Kim Novak switched off the Puch. She straddled it for a moment with her feet on the gravel, smiling and taking in the 108 students standing as still as statues in the playground. Then she climbed off, elegantly flipped out the kick-stand, took a flat briefcase from the rack, and marched right through the petrified crowd and into the school.

When she was out of sight, I noticed Edmund was standing beside me. Nearly shoulder to shoulder, though he was a bit taller.

When he spoke, his voice was thick with emotion.

'That's what I call a mature woman.'

I nodded, thinking of his dad's girlie mags. I reckoned he knew what he was talking about.

Within two hours, we'd got to the bottom of it. Those who kept to the football-side of the school had long known that Bertil 'Berra' Albertsson was moving to town; we might have worked it out as well if we'd given some thought to what we'd read in the local news. Berra was a handball legend who had competed in over 150 international matches. It was said that his shots were so hard that goalies died when they were hit in the head. After twelve seasons in the All-Swedish and national teams, he was going to wind things down by becoming a player-coach for our town's handball team, with the aim of taking it to the top of the league. Even someone like Veikko knew what this meant, and we'd all read about it in *Kurren* a few weeks ago. Super-Berra was going to move into one of the newly built houses over in Ångermanland, and he was taking up his post as vice president of parks on the first of July.

What wasn't in the papers was that he was engaged to Kim Novak, and that her name was actually Ewa Kaludis.

And that she'd be standing in for hopeless old Eleonora Sintring, who had broken her femur while spring-boarding over a plinth during Housewives' Gymnastics earlier that month.

The day after Ewa Kaludis arrived, several football players

passed around a volunteer sign-up sheet that you could add your name to if you were willing to break Sintring's other leg when she came back to work. The idea was that all the willing participants would then draw straws to see who would do the deed.

By the time Benny and I wrote our names down, the list was already several pages long.

The next Saturday I bumped into Edmund in the library.

'Do you come here often?' I asked.

'Sometimes,' said Edmund. 'Quite often, actually. I read a lot.'

It might have been true. I came here once a month at most, so I wasn't surprised that we hadn't run into each other here before. After all, Edmund was relatively new in town.

'What do you like to read?' I asked.

'Crime,' he answered without hesitation. 'Stagge and Quentin and Carter Dickson.'

I nodded. I hadn't heard of any of them.

'Jules Verne, too,' he added after a pause.

'Jules Verne is damn good,' I said.

'Damn good,' said Edmund.

We stood around avoiding each other's eyes.

'What about the summer?' he then asked.

'What about it?' I said.

'With that place,' Edmund said. 'Your house.'

I couldn't see where he was going with this.

'Huh?' I said.

He removed his glasses and adjusted the tape that held them together. This time he seemed to have broken them at the bridge.

'Shit,' he said.

I didn't answer. There was a long silence.

'Can I come or not?' he finally said.

'Can I?' I said. 'What do you mean?'

He sighed.

'Well, shit, you're the one who gets to decide if I can come with you,' he said.

And then the penny dropped. Suddenly I felt ashamed. Goosebumps prickled my spine.

'Too damn right you can,' I said.

Edmund put his glasses on.

'Are you sure?'

'Of course I am,' I said. The goosebumps vanished. There was a pause.

'Cool,' he said then, with the same thick voice he'd used in the playground. 'Umm, do you prefer Märklin or Fleischman trains?'

3

Henry, my brother, was a beanpole. Everyone said so.

He was handsome, too; at least that's what women said. Personally, I didn't have an eye for men's looks at the time, but he did remind me of Ricky Nelson, and I assumed that was a good thing.

Or Rick, as he was called as of the previous year.

Henry smoked Lucky Strikes. He pulled them out of the breast pocket of his white nylon shirt with a gesture that indicated he had been working hard, goddammit, and it was time to regroup with a smoke.

The year before our mother ended up on her deathbed, he'd bought his first car—the family's first car, in fact: a black VW Beetle that he drove around in when he was reporting from the countryside. He'd bought a camera, too, so he could take pictures of accidents and the 'victims' of his interviews. I was under the impression that things were going well with the freelancing.

Our father used to say so: 'He's getting along well, our Henry.'

I didn't really know what was meant by the term 'freelance'. Henry only seemed to be writing for *Kurren*, but that word was intertwined with the others. Lucky Strike. Beat. Freelance. He'd christened the VW Beetle 'Killer'.

The next Sunday morning, we were sitting in the kitchen.

'Hey, Erik.'

'Yes, Henry?'

Killer was parked out on Idrottsgatan. He'd lit a Lucky and was slurping the lukewarm dregs of the coffee Dad had left behind before he took the bus to the hospital.

'We're mucking in together this summer.'

'That's what I hear.'

He took a drag.

'It's probably the best thing for you.'

I nodded and looked out of the window. The sun was shining brightly. On a day like this, you could swim in Möckeln.

'This situation with Mum ... it's horrible,' said Henry.

'Definitely,' I said.

With his elbows still perched the table, he leaned back a bit and looked out at the sunshine.

'Nice day.'

I nodded.

'We could go for a spin and check the place out.'

'Sure,' I said.

'Are you up for it?'

'I don't have anything else to do,' I said.

Henry and I did some sorting out in Gennesaret that Sunday. We tidied up and prepared for the summer. We dragged all the mattresses and pillows and blankets on to the lawn so the sun could draw out the winter's damp. We aired the house and swept the floors. Upstairs and down. There wasn't really that much to do. On the ground floor there were two rooms and a small kitchen with a basin that drained into a dry well, a refrigerator and a stove. To get to the top floor you walked up a stairway on the gable wall. Two rooms in a row. A slanted roof.

When the sun was out, it was scorching up there.

We also had a swim. The jetty was in its usual spot at the southern end of the point. Henry said he'd turn it into a floating dock this year. I nodded and said that it was a damn good idea.

But we'll need better planks, Henry said.

We sunbathed on the mattresses and chatted. Well, actually, we smoked. Henry gave me two Luckys and swore he'd wallop me if I told Dad.

I had no intention of saying anything anyway. We drove home in the middle of the afternoon, during the hottest part of the day. Henry had a football game to watch that night. We brought both propane tanks with us, the one for the stove and the one for the refrigerator, so we could get them refilled in time for the holidays.

Overall, it was a good Sunday, and I thought it might turn out to be a bearable summer, after all.

Difficult, but bearable.

I was more interested in Edmund's dad's magazines than I was in Edmund's Fleischmann, but I didn't let on.

Edmund's room was around eight square metres in size and the fibreboard sheet holding the railway took up about six of them. All in all it was well organized. He slept on a bed under the sheet, where he also had a lamp, a bookshelf and a few drawers with clothes. I didn't see any Wild West magazines.

'Should we rebuild it?' said Edmund.

'Okay,' I said.

We rearranged the whole landscape in two hours, drove the train around, and orchestrated some nifty crashes until we grew bored.

'Building it up is the most fun,' said Edmund. 'After that, it just sits there.'

'Agreed,' I said.

'One of my cousins gave it to me,' said Edmund. 'He got married and his wife wouldn't let him keep it.'

'Well,' I said. 'That's how the cookie crumbles.'

'You have to choose your old lady carefully,' said Edmund. 'Should we go to the kitchen and have a Pommac?'

We had a Pommac in Edmund's kitchen and I wanted to ask him about the girlie mags and about him having twelve toes instead of ten, but I never quite found the right moment.

Instead, we cycled home to Idrottsgatan and had an old apple juice. I took Edmund into the woods, too, and showed him the culvert. He thought it was dead cool—at least, that's what he said. Then he realized that he was half an hour late for dinner, and we both went home.

Stava School's staffroom was on the girls' end of the third floor. It featured a sizable balcony, the only one on the building, and as summer approached the teachers often sat up there under colourful parasols, drinking coffee and smoking. We never actually saw them from the playground, but we heard them arguing and laughing and we could see their clouds of smoke billowing.

During Ewa Kaludis's brief sojourn at the school, the behaviour on the balcony had changed quite a bit. People had started to stand while smoking instead of sitting. They leaned over the railing and stared vacantly across the playground. She was the first to do that, and of course the studs crowded around her, puffing away and grinning.

Stensjöö, the deputy head teacher, Håkansson the Horse. Brylle.

'Check out bloody Brylle,' said Benny. 'He's giving it to her from behind.'

'Rubbish,' said Balthazar Lindblom. 'They wouldn't dare. Look but don't touch, right? If they even brushed up against her, Super-Berra would come down here and beat them up.'

'Too right,' said Veikko. 'He'd just knock their heads off with a ball. What a geezer.'

The girls' side was unusually crowded during those days in late May. Quite a few football players seemed to have developed nobler interests, and the bike shed was packed. Ewa Kaludis only taught our class and one other, so most kids had to grab any opportunity they got to gawk at her.

Like during breaks when she was up on the balcony. Kim Novak. Ewa Kaludis. Super-Berra's super-girl.

I was one of the lucky ones. We'd had the hopeless Sintring in English and Geography before she stumbled over the plinth. Håkansson the Horse had jumped in and covered for her for a few weeks, but now Ewa Kaludis had been inflicted on us. With only three weeks until the summer holidays. It was pure torment.

Sweet torment.

She didn't have to teach us. It wasn't necessary. We worked like dogs anyway. Whenever she entered the classroom, we sat in rapt silence. She would smile and her eyes twinkled. It gave us all the chills. Then she would sit down on the teacher's desk, cross one leg over the other and tell us to keep working on one page or another. Her voice reminded me of a purring cat.

We worked diligently. Ewa Kaludis either sat on her desk,

sparkling, or walked around swivelling her hips as she moved between the desks. If you raised your hand, she'd almost always stand behind you, a little off to the side. When she leaned forward, her breasts would rest against your shoulder. Or, rather, one of her breasts would. It seemed that the boys were always in need of help, and the air in the classroom was heavy with her perfume and with youthful, suppressed desire.

I didn't really know what the girls thought of Ewa Kaludis, because I never talked to them, but I reckoned that they benefited from her presence as well. In their own female way. But I could be wrong. Maybe they were green with envy.

Once when I raised my hand and she came over to help, I felt her breast brush against both my shoulder and my cheek and I almost fainted. I began to black out, and I thought that if I died right then, it would be a happy death.

She noticed, I think, because she put her hand on my arm and asked me how I was feeling. Of course, that only made matters worse, but then I bit my tongue and things became clearer.

'I'm not feeling very well,' I said. 'I think I'm getting my period.'

I have no idea why I said that, but Ewa Kaludis just laughed. Benny, who was sitting next to me and was the only other person who heard my brilliant remark, said he'd never bloody heard anything like it.

'Fucking hell, Erik. You'll be sitting pretty after that. You can count on it.'

I wasn't sure that he was right, but mostly I was relieved that she didn't get angry.

'Let's wait a moment,' my father said. 'They're not quite done with their rounds.'

I nodded, hugging the bag filled with grapes from Pressbyrån, the corner shop, wrinkling it even more.

'Don't crush the grapes,' my father said.

'I won't,' I said.

We sat in silence on the green benches. Nurses whizzed by and smiled benignly at us.

'The rounds always take time,' said my father. 'They have a lot on.'

'I know.'

'You have time to go comb your hair. There's a loo over there in the corner.'

I went and combed my hair with my new steel comb. I had broken off five of the teeth from the slim end so I could pick the locks on the loos at the railway station. It didn't work, but that wasn't the point. The important thing was that I had a steel comb and it had those teeth missing. If you were a girls-sider and didn't have a steel comb, you were worth less than a burst bicycle tube. It was what it was.

'We can go in soon,' said my father when I came back out.

'I know,' I said. 'But there's no rush.'

'You're right about that,' said my father.

She tried to hug me, but I caressed her arm instead, which was just as good. My father sat to her right, and I to her left.

'We brought some grapes,' said my father.

'Lovely,' said my mother.

I put the Pressbyrån bag on top of the yellow hospital blanket.

'How's school?' asked my mother.

'Good,' I said.

'You're taking the day off?'

'Yes.'

She peered into the bag and then closed it again.

'And how are things at home?'

'No problems there,' I said. 'Dad burns the gravy sometimes, but he's getting better every day.'

My mother smiled and, as if that were very taxing, she closed her eyes. I looked at her. Her face was greyish-blue and her hair looked like wan grass.

'No problems,' I repeated. 'Is there a loo here?'

'Of course,' said my mother in a tired voice. 'It's out in the corridor.'

I nodded and walked out. I tried to shit to no avail for twenty-five minutes, and then I went back in.

My mother and father were sitting very close to each other, whispering. They fell silent when they noticed me come in. I sat on the chair to her left.

'Are you going to Gennesaret soon?' my mother asked.

'Yes, we are,' I said. 'Henry and I have already been over and put things in order.'

'I'm glad that Emmy and Henry are taking care of you.'

'Yes,' I said.

'Henry's getting along well,' my father said.

There was a pause.

'It was nice of you to visit,' said my mother.

'Oh, it's no bother,' I said.

'I think we'll get going now,' said my father. 'So we can catch the quarter-past bus.'

'Do,' said my mother. 'I don't need anything here.'

'I'll come by tomorrow after work,' said my father.

'No need,' said my mother.

I got up and patted her on the forearm and left.

I took out the Colonel Darkin books and counted them. Yes, right. Six of them. Six black waxed-paper notebooks with forty-eight pages in each. Five of the notebooks were finished; the sixth was almost done and dusted.

I stuffed the completed adventures back into the plastic bag and pushed them far inside my underwear drawer. It wasn't an ideal hiding place; I had often thought of finding something better—maybe I could bury them in a bag out in the forest. Further along in the dry ditch: they would be as safe as houses there.

But I hadn't got around to it. Of course, the underwear drawer was much safer now that my mother was in hospital. My father wasn't the one who rooted around in my things. He hardly ever came into my room at all.

I'd created Colonel Darkin about two years ago. Linda-Britt, my fat buck-toothed cousin, had given me one of those notebooks as a birthday present because she thought I should keep a diary. She told me she kept one herself and found it very enriching.

There weren't even any lines in the book, which was strange since she wanted me to write in it. So I used a ruler and divided each page up like a comic book, four panels per side, all on the right hand side of the page, forty-eight parts; and with that I was on my way with *Colonel Darkin and the Golden Gang*. It was an adventure story set between London, Askersund and the Wild West, and it contained everything you could ask for from double-crossing and incorruptible honour to razor-sharp dialogue.

'You have exactly one second to give me an answer, Mr. Frege, my time is valuable.'

'That's a mighty fine body you have there, Miss Carlson. Do you want to keep it?'

'By the antlers of a moose, Nessie, you forgot to spike the tea with rum.'

Colonel Darkin himself was a scarred sleuth who'd retreated to his log cabin in the mountains, and only poked his head out when the world needed him. His busty blonde niece was his sidekick, and she held sway over the opposite sex. I named her Vera Lane, and from her very first panel, I was in love.

At the moment, she was locked away in an attic tower belonging to a mad scientist called Finckelberg. He had just roared off into town in his Ferrari to buy petrol so he could set her on fire. One hundred kilometres in the distance, Darkin was speeding toward the tower on his motorcycle, a BSA 300 LT with diamond spokes. I had to make sure he reached her before the flames began to lap at her lovely body; but I only had eight pages left in the notebook, and I was rubbish at drawing fire.

I knew perfectly well that I wasn't a particularly talented comic-book artist, but I felt a certain responsibility to the characters I'd created. If I didn't write about them and keep drawing them, they would just sit there in the underwear drawer like forgotten marionettes.

Sometimes it felt like a chore. But for the most part—especially when I was on a roll—it was one of the most meaningful things that I did during my entire childhood. Perhaps it felt that way because those were the only times that I managed to leave the troubles of the world behind.

I'd never shown them to another living soul. And I'd never told anyone about Colonel Darkin.

It was that kind of hobby.

I opened an apple juice, took two large gulps. I thought for a while.

'Goddammit!' I wrote in Colonel Darkin's speech bubble. 'I should've known there'd be a catch.'

4

Henry, my brother, wrote about everything in *Kurren*.

About city-council meetings, speedway contests, and suspected arson. About two-headed calves and siblings meeting for the first time after fifty-seven years. What he didn't glean from the news desk or from the local area, he found in other newspapers, both Swedish and international. He spent at least an hour a day in the Örebro library skimming the news and sensational headlines from all over the world, looking for leads for his own stories.

He cut out everything he'd written that had made it to print and glued the clippings into large scrapbooks. At this point, during the summer that our mother was going to die, he already had half a dozen he sometimes let me leaf through when I visited his bedsit on Grevgatan. I liked curling up in his sagging bed, which had iron bars on the short ends of the frame, and perusing the headlines. I rarely read the articles, but the headlines spoke to me; at that time I didn't know that it was usually someone other than Henry who came up with these beauties: 'Sly Stowaway Sow Travels 200 Km'; 'Schnapps: Good for Your Blood Pressure'; 'German Ministers on French Leave in Arboga'.

After I read a great headline, I would close my eyes and try to picture the complicated reality hidden behind it.

Sometimes I could, sometimes not.

'One thing,' said Henry, my brother, one day when there was less than a week left of spring semester.

I looked up from a cutting about a fireman from Flen who had fractured both femurs in Frövi.

'Yeah?' I said.

Henry studied his cigarette and then put it out in the wet sand inside the monkey's skull that he kept next to his Facit Privat typewriter.

'About the summer.'

He's backing out, I thought. What a tosser.

'What about it?' I said.

'A couple of things, really,' he said and looked more like Ricky Nelson than ever. Or Rick, rather. I closed the scrapbook.

'I'm taking time off from *Kurren*.'

'Mm?'

'The whole summer.'

'The whole summer?'

'That's right. I'm going to write a book.'

It was as if he were talking about going to Karlesson's to buy an ice lolly.

'A book?' I said.

'Yep. It has to happen some time.'

'Oh?'

'Some people have no choice in the matter. I'm one of those people.'

I nodded. I was sure that he was. I didn't really know what to say.

'What's it going to be about?'

He didn't answer right away. He put his feet up on his desk, took a gulp of Rio Club from the bottle on the floor and fished out a fresh Lucky Strike.

'Life,' he said. 'The real thing. Existentially speaking.'

'Aha,' I said.

He lit his cigarette and we sat in silence. Henry took a few long drags, his shoulder blades resting on the back of the chair. He stared up at the ceiling where the smoke was thinning out into nothing.

'Good,' I said finally. 'It's cool that you're writing a book. I reckon it'll be bloody great.'

He didn't seem to care what I had to say.

'Was there anything else?' I asked.

'Like what?' said Henry.

'You said there were a couple of things. The book, that's just one, right?'

'Oh, you're a devil with numbers, brother,' said Henry. 'A right bloody calculator.'

'At least when it comes to counting to two,' I said.

Henry laughed. He had a short laugh that was sort of sharp. It sounded cool and I had tried to mimic it, too, but it didn't really work. Laughs were hard to learn, I had found out.

'Well, it's about Emmy,' said Henry and then he blew a ring of smoke that soared through the room like a sputnik.

'Brill,' I said when it hit the wall and dissipated. 'What about Emmy?'

'She's not coming,' said Henry.

'What?' I said.

'She's not coming to Gennesaret.'

'Why not?'

'I dumped her,' said Henry.

I wasn't sure what that meant. Unless he meant that he had beaten her to death and thrown her into a canal with her feet encased in cement blocks, and that didn't seem likely. Vera

Lane had been close to getting this treatment in *Darkin III*, but I couldn't imagine Henry doing something like that.

'Oh no,' I said, trying to sound neutral.

'So it's just going to be you and me and your mate. What's his name?'

'Edmund,' I said.

'Edmund?' said Henry. 'Bloody hell, what a name.'

'He's okay,' I said.

'Sure, sure,' said Henry. 'You can't judge a person by their name. I banged a bird called Frida Arsel once. In Amsterdam. She wasn't bad at all.'

I nodded and sat a while, thinking about all the birds with strange names that I'd banged.

And all the birds I'd dumped.

'Let's keep Dad and Mum in the dark,' said Henry.

'What do you mean?'

'I don't want them to know that Emmy won't be joining us. They'll only worry about us not being able to feed ourselves and what not,' said my brother Henry. 'But we will. Three lads in their prime.'

'You know it,' I said. 'No problem. I'm a wiz with omelettes.'

And then Henry laughed his sharp laugh again. It felt good. It occurred to me that when my brother laughed, it was as comforting as being scratched on the back.

One day during the last week of school we went on a class trip to Brumberga Wildlife Park. I stuck with Edmund, Benny and Arse-Enok the whole time, and even though an all-girls' team beat us at the quiz by one single rotten point and we lost out on the litre of ice cream, we had a pretty rewarding afternoon. Arse-Enok had just had his birthday and had raked in a whole fifty-kronor note from his dim-witted uncle, so we were rolling in it. Arse-Enok wasn't one to hold back. He wolfed down fifty-four Dixi caramels and had to sit in one of the sick-seats on the ride home.

I ate thirty-six Reval sweets myself and felt brilliant.

The following night I had a dream. I was at the wildlife park again and the whole class was standing in front of a large green aquarium with dolphins, rays and seals. Sharks, too, I think. None of us moved a muscle or said a word, because Ewa Kaludis was speaking. Behind her, the large torpedo-like bodies continued their endless journey round and round in the green water.

Then Benny swore. I saw at once what he was pointing at with his dirty index finger.

My mother was floating by in the aquarium.

Among the rays and seals. My mother.

It made me feel awful. She was wearing her worn blue house dress, the one with the bleached-out roses, and she looked swollen and bug-eyed. I rushed toward the glass, gesturing at her to move to the other side, but she just hung there in the water and stared at us with her sad eyes. It seemed impossible to get her to move, so I turned around, pressed myself against the glass and spread out my arms, trying to hide her. Ewa Kaludis fell silent and gave me a curious look. She seemed disappointed, and I wanted to cry and wet myself and be swallowed up by the earth.

When I woke up it was quarter to five in the morning and I was soaked through with a cold sweat. I thought it must have something to do with the Reval caramels. I got out of bed and sat on the toilet but it was pointless.

As I sat there I thought about the dream. It was weird. Brumberga Wildlife Park didn't have an aquarium, and Ewa

44

Kaludis hadn't even been on the trip with us.

I didn't get to sleep again that night.

Just before I walked into the flat, Edmund said: 'Do you know what the biggest difference in the world is between?'

'The universe and Åsa Lenner's brain?' I said.

'Nope,' said Edmund. 'It's between my dad and my mum. Just so you know.'

Over the course of the dinner they had invited me to, I saw that he wasn't wrong. It was a sort of pre-thank you for letting Edmund stay at Gennesaret all summer, I think.

Albin Wester, Edmund's father, was short and stocky, with limp arms and a rolling gait. He looked like a silverback. A bit worn-out and resigned, too; even though I was an anti-footballer, I was reminded of a football coach trying to come up with a strategy during half-time when the team was down 6–0. Upbeat, yet resigned. He talked throughout the meal, especially when his mouth was full.

Mrs. Wester looked as severe as a longcase Mora clock draped in a mourning shroud. She didn't say a word during dinner, but she tried to muster a smile every so often. And when she did, she seemed on the verge of cracking, and then she'd hiccup and squeeze her eyes shut.

'Have more, boys,' said Albin Wester. 'You never know when you'll get your next meal. Signe's sausage bake is famous across northern Europe.'

Both Edmund and I ate heartily, because it was extremely tasty. I thought of the domestic situation facing us that summer and told Edmund to ask his mum to give us the recipe.

I knew that kind of gesture was considered the height of good manners, and as if on cue the Mora clock cracked open and hiccupped.

'Sausage Bake à la Signe,' said Albin Wester out of the corner of his mouth. 'Food fit for the gods.'

He smiled, too, and a few pieces of sausage fell in his lap.

'She's an alcoholic,' Edmund explained afterward. 'It takes every muscle in her body to get through a dinner like this.'

I thought that sounded strange and said so. Edmund shrugged.

'Eh,' he said. 'It's not strange at all. She has three sisters. They're all the same. They're like Grandpa—that man drank like a fish—but the female body can't seem to take it.'

'Yeah?' I said.

'You shouldn't give womenfolk schnapps. Or put gunpowder in their tobacco. It's too much for them.'

'You sound like Salasso,' I said. 'Do you read lots of Wild West magazines?'

'Sometimes,' said Edmund. 'But lately I've been reading more books.'

'I like to mix it up,' I said diplomatically. 'How long has she been like that, by the way? Can't you make her better?'

I wasn't entirely unfamiliar with the ills of alcohol. My father's cousin Holger was of that type and in fourth grade we'd had a teacher for half a semester who went by the name Finkel-Jesus. He drank steadily in the classroom throughout the day and was fired after he fell asleep in the staffroom and pissed himself.

Rumour has it, in any case.

Edmund shook his head.

'We keep it in the family,' he said. 'It's not officious.'

'Uh-huh,' I said. 'But I think the word is "official".'

'Who cares what it's called,' said Edmund. 'Either way, she's why we move so often. At least, I think so.'

And then I felt sorry for Edmund Wester.

And for his dad.

And maybe I felt a bit sorry for Mrs. Wester, too.

We went to see a Jerry Lewis film at the Saga that evening. The Westers treated us to that, too.

'Holy shit,' Edmund said while we walked home. 'Everyone should be like Jerry Lewis. Then the world would be fab.'

'If everyone was like Jerry Lewis,' I said, 'then the world would have gone to the dogs thousands of years ago.'

'Clever,' he said. 'We do need Perry Mason types, too; you're absolutely right.'

'Paul Drake and Della,' I said.

'Paul Drake is too bloody good,' said Edmund. 'The way he walks into the courtroom in the middle of a cross-examination and winks at Perry. Christ, what a bloke!'

'And he always wears a white blazer and black trousers,' I said. 'Or maybe it's the other way around.'

'Always,' said Edmund.

'Della is in love with him,' I said.

'Objection,' said Edmund. 'Della is in love with Perry.'

'The hell she is,' I said. 'She's in love with Paul Drake.'

'Okay,' said Edmund. 'She's in love with both of them. That's not so odd.'

'That's why she can't choose between them,' I said. 'Objection sustained.'

We went around saying those lines for a while.

'Objection overruled.'

'Objection sustained.'

'Cross-examine the witness.'

'No further questions, your honour.'

'Not guilty!'

Edmund lived further up on Mossbanegatan and I lived down by the sports centre, so we went our separate ways at Karlesson's shop. Karlesson's was closed for the evening; its green windows were shut and the chewing-gum dispenser was chained to the bike rack and locked with a padlock.

'Did you know you can use broken sausage forks in the gum dispenser?' I asked Edmund.

'What?' said Edmund. 'What do you mean?'

I explained. You simply broke a centimetre off the end of the flat wooden spoons they give out with mash. Ice cream spoons worked too, actually, but they were harder to find. Then you pushed the wooden bit into the twenty-five-öre slot and gave it a turn. No problem. Clickety clickety click. Shake shake. Worked every time.

'You're kidding,' said Edmund. 'Are you up for it?'

We dug around in the rubbish bin that was mounted to the wall and finally found a sticky ice-cream spoon. I measured and broke it off against my thumbnail. We waited for a gang of giggling girls to pass by, and then we did the deed.

Four balls and one ring.

We each took two balls and Edmund took the ring for his alcoholic mother.

'Slick,' said Edmund. 'We should come here one night this summer and clean it out.'

I nodded. I'd been harbouring that plan for a while.

'You just have to find the spoons,' I said. 'But there're always some on the ground near the hot-dog stands. Herman's and Törner's on the square.'

'One of these nights, we'll do it,' said Edmund.

'Sustained,' I said. 'One night this summer.'

Then we said goodbye.

I knew that my brother Henry was an unusual person, but I didn't know just how unusual until he said something one evening; it must have also been during the final week of school.

'Super-Berra is a cunt,' he said.

I had mentioned him. Or Ewa Kaludis, rather, and so I'd probably said something about her being with Berra.

'Like I said, a right cunt.'

It was just a statement; I was so surprised I didn't know how to respond and then we started to talk about something else and then Henry left for a Maranatha meeting in Killer.

After he'd gone, I wondered why he'd even say something like that, and then I remembered that he'd interviewed Bertil Albertsson once for *Kurren*, when he'd moved to town in early May.

Super-Berra: a cunt?

I wrote it on a piece of paper and stuck it in *Colonel Darkin and the Golden Lamb*. The statement was so remarkable that I wanted to preserve it somehow.

Later in the summer I'd have reason to reflect on this moment. A big reason. But I didn't know that then, and the scrap of paper must have disappeared somehow, because I never saw it again.

5

This year was our last real graduation ceremony of primary school.

Some of the class would go on to eighth grade, as well; about half of us would transfer to KCJSS, the Kumla County Junior Secondary School, in the autumn. Those of us who hadn't quit after sixth grade, that is. It was a milestone; among other things I would never again sit in the same classroom as Veikko and Sluggo and Gunborg and Balthazar Lindblom.

It didn't really matter, but I'd miss a few of them. Benny and Marie-Louise, for instance. Well, Benny I'd see in the culvert and around town, but I'd never again be able to sit and fantasize about Marie-Louise and her lovely dark locks and brown eyes. At least not at close range.

But I'd get over it. I'd never really made any progress with Marie-Louise anyway. I was sure there would be new foxy chicks in the secondary school. And if you missed your chance with one, there'd be a thousand others to take her place. *C'est la vie.*

But how would I live without Ewa Kaludis? This question suddenly—and unhappily—opened up like an abyss. It was as if her breast had stayed pressed against my shoulder since I told her that I was getting my period. Ewa visited our classroom on graduation day just as Brylle was opening the present that the girls had bought him: a large framed picture of a glum moose standing at the edge of a forest. Everyone knew that Brylle hunted moose for a week every autumn, and now he was standing there behind his desk staring at the picture, forcing a wide smile.

'I just want to thank you all for the time we shared,' said Ewa Kaludis. 'It has been a pleasure to teach you. I hope you have a good summer break.'

By light years, it was the most spiritual thing I'd heard in my fourteen-year-old life. Her hips swayed as she left the room and an ice-cold hand gripped my heart.

Damn it, I thought. Is this how she's going to leave me? Sitting at my desk, I was paralyzed by a sudden realization: This is what it's like to lose something invaluable. This is how it must feel five seconds before you throw yourself in front of a train.

As luck would have it, no train rolled through the classroom.

'What's with you?' said Benny when we were basking in the sunshine on the playground. 'You look bloody punch-drunk. Like Henry Cooper in the twelfth round.'

'Oh,' I said. 'It's just my stomach. When are you off?'

'In two hours,' said Benny. 'I'll get there tomorrow morning. It's a long bloody way to Malmberget. I hope the thing with your mum gets better.'

'I'm sure it will,' I said.

'I'm going down to Blidberg's to buy a Bonanza shirt,' Benny said. 'And one of those red bloody ties—I've got to impress the cousins. See you in the autumn.'

'Say hi to those Lapp-buggers and to the mosquitoes for me,' I said.

'You know I will,' said Benny. 'Write to me if it turns out to be a difficult summer.'

My brother Henry had already installed himself at Gennesaret. As far as my father knew, Emmy Kaskel was with him, but of course I knew better. The idea was that Edmund and I would cycle the twenty-five kilometres there on Sunday and join them. Henry could've given us a lift, of course, but leaving our bikes behind was out of the question. There were plenty of interesting places to explore in the forests around Möckeln. Without our bikes, we'd be like cowboys without their trusty steeds; that's what Edmund and I both thought.

On the Saturday night my father and I visited the hospital again, me in my graduation outfit, Dad in a blazer, shirt and tie. He never wore a tie at work or around the house, but when he went to the hospital, he dressed up. Even though he rode the bus there more or less every day. I wondered why, but I never wanted to ask. I didn't want to that day either.

My mother lay in the same bed in the same room and seemed mostly unchanged. Her hair was newly washed and looked a bit better. Like a halo on her pillow.

We'd brought a bag of fresh grapes and a bar of chocolate, but after an hour with her, as we were leaving, she foisted the chocolate on me.

'Take it, Erik,' she said. 'You need to put some meat on your bones.'

I didn't want it, but I took it anyway.

'I hope you have a good time at Gennesaret,' said my mother.

'You know I will,' I said. 'Take care.'

'Send my regards to Henry and Emmy,' she said.

'I will,' I said.

On the bus home, my dad talked a lot about what we could and couldn't do at Gennesaret. What we should try to bear in mind and what we absolutely mustn't forget. The propane, among other things. He was trying to hide the note that he was holding in his hand. Presumably it was something my mother had written and had given to him during our visit while I was in the bathroom. I could tell by his tone that he didn't really care about the advice he was giving. He trusted Henry and Emmy. He rambled on out of duty and empathy with Mum. I felt sorry for him.

I think he trusted me, too, actually.

'I might pop by some time,' he said. 'And you'll come to town every now and then, won't you?'

I nodded, knowing that these were mostly just things you say to make yourself feel better.

'But I'm working three more weeks. And I'll want to visit her at the weekends.'

It was strange that he said 'her' instead of 'Ellen' or 'your mother', as he usually did.

'It is what it is,' I said. 'We'll be fine.'

I took out the chocolate bar—a Tarragona—the one that had been for my mother, but that she'd given back to me. I handed it to my dad.

'Do you want some?' I said.

He shook his head.

'You take it. I don't fancy it.'

I put it back in the inner pocket of my jacket. We sat in silence as we passed through Mosås, past the peat-moss bog where Henry had worked for a couple of summers before he went to sea; I tried to picture Ewa Kaludis's face, but I couldn't quite.

'If you find the time, tar the boat,' said my father when we turned toward town at the junction. 'It couldn't hurt.'

'Sure,' I said.

'The jetty isn't up to much, I suppose.'

'We'll fix that, too.'

'If you have the time,' said my father and tucked away the paper my mother had given him. 'And then the rest is up to you.'

'Only time will tell,' I said.

'Keep your chin up, and your feet on the ground,' said my father.

When we got off the bus at Mossbanegatan, I furtively tossed the Tarragona into the rubbish bin that hung on the bus stop post.

I regretted it all the way home to Idrottsgatan, but I didn't go back to get it.

A man's gotta do what a man's gotta do, I thought.

It alternated between sunshine and clouds on the Sunday as Edmund and I left town. A gentle headwind. When we pedalled through Hallsberg it started to rain and so we went into Lampa's bakery outside the station and each had a Pommac and a cinnamon bun. Edmund tossed a krona into the jukebox. While we sat and drank our Pommacs and stared out at the rain, we listened to 'Cotton Fields' three times in a row. There were no other tunes in the jukebox that were worth playing, Edmund said, and I took him at his word.

And 'Cotton Fields' was a cracking song.

I had warned Edmund about the Kleva hill, but that had only made him even more determined to perform a grand feat on this, the first day of our summer holiday.

'I'll do the whole thing in one go,' he said. 'I'll put fifty öre on it.'

'I'll give you one krona,' I said because I knew what was going to happen. 'There's no chance you'll make it over Kleva without a racing bike.'

Both Edmund and I had second-hand bicycles without any embellishments other than baskets and bells. No banana seats. No gears. No brakes on the handlebars. At least Edmund's was a Crescent. Mine was a pale green Ferm, and it was nothing to write home about.

'I'm going to give it a good go,' declared Edmund as the hill came into view. 'No further questions.'

He made it almost halfway up. And then we had to sit on the roadside for fifteen minutes until Edmund's legs would start to obey him again. A light froth had formed at the corners of his mouth. He lay on his back on the bank, legs shaking, his bike beside him.

'Bloody bugger of a hill,' he groaned. 'When we lived in Sveg there was a real killer there, but this one was much worse, I tell you. I was a little bit sick over there, don't sit in it.'

He pointed and I lay down at a safe distance. I clasped my hands behind my neck and squinted at the sky as I watched the billowing clouds roll by. Edmund was still breathing heavily and seemed to have trouble speaking, so we lay like this for a few minutes and sort of just *were*.

Were on the edge of the road halfway up the Kleva hill. One Sunday in June 1962.

This would have been impossible to do with Benny; it would've been impossible to simply lie still. We would've surely been smoking and swearing, but with Edmund I didn't have to say a word and it didn't feel strange at all.

Not this time—when he was about to faint from lactic acidosis—and not the next times either. Talking was optional; it was that simple. I couldn't put my finger on why. Was it because his mother was an alcoholic or because he'd lived in Norrland for so long? It didn't matter. The point was that it could be this way; Edmund's silence was a good thing and I decided to tell him this when I knew him better.

In a few days or so.

Henry had picked up at least sixteen tins of Ulla-Bella's meatballs in brown gravy for a song at Laxman's—the supermarket in Åsbro, a village that lay a few kilometres away from Gennesaret—and on the first night we ate two of them along with potatoes in their jackets and lingonberries that Henry had brought with him from town. We had a choice of milk or apple juice.

It tasted fine. Edmund and I did the washing up while Henry sat outside on one of the sun loungers with his coffee and cigarettes. Occasionally he jotted down a few lines in the writing pad on his lap while nodding to himself.

Later in the evening he clattered on the Facit's keys at the desk in his room. I could tell that the book was being born. The one about life. The real deal.

And I could see that this was how it was going to be.

Ulla-Bella's meatballs with potatoes and lingonberries.

Henry and the existential novel.

Edmund and I doing the washing up.

'We're living the good life,' said Edmund when we were almost finished. He sounded moved, and I agreed with him.

'It could be worse,' I said.

But of course Henry had more ideas about how things should be. From the start, it was clear that he'd take the bedroom on the ground floor and that Edmund and I would sleep on the top floor. This wasn't something we needed to discuss. Neither was the fact that the three of us would have a free run of the kitchen and the main room.

'Except,' said Henry.

'Except what?' I said.

'Except if I pull a bird one night. Then you'll have to stay away from the ground floor.'

'That's a given,' I said.

'A gentleman's agreement,' said Edmund.

'You cook every other day, and so do I. Just dinner, and no baby portions. Same goes for the washing up. Okay?'

'Okay,' we said.

'We shop at Laxman's. I'll go in Killer, but if you like you can cycle or take the boat.'

We nodded. No problem.

'The bog,' Henry then said.

'The bog,' we said and sighed.

'The less we shit, the better,' said Henry. 'And no one gets to piss in it, it's bloody bad manners. If we look after it, we can get away with emptying it every other week. You know how it works, Erik … dig a hole, take it out, empty it. I know, there are better jobs. Okay?'

We nodded again.

'That's all,' said Henry. 'Let's not make life unnecessarily complicated. It should be like a butterfly on a summer's day.'

That last bit sounded good. I mulled it over.

Life should be like a butterfly on a summer's day.

One month was left until the Incident.

'So, about your toes,' I said when we went to bed that first night. 'What's the story?'

Our beds were arranged in the only way possible. Each along our own wall, with the slanted ceiling so close you couldn't sit up. About a metre apart, and a chest of drawers with our clothes inside and masses of comics and books on top. Edmund had sent five shoeboxes of magazines and one bag of books with Henry.

'My toes?' said Edmund.

'I heard people talking,' I said.

'Oh?' said Edmund and giggled. 'You can barely see anything any more.' He thrust his left foot out and wiggled his toes. 'How many do you see?'

'I count five,' I said. 'Pretty ugly.'

'Correct,' said Edmund. 'But when I had six, they were even uglier, so they took one away.'

'Who?' I said.

'The doctors, of course,' said Edmund. 'If you look at the index toe or whatever it's called, you can see a small scar. That's where the extra one was.'

I got on my knees on the floor and examined Edmund's dirty left foot. He was right. Almost at the base of the big toe I could see a small, delicate scratch, thin as a pencil mark and not more than a centimetre long.

I nodded and crawled back into bed.

'Cheers,' I said. 'I just wanted to see.'

'No worries,' said Edmund and pulled his foot back under the blanket. 'Do you want to see the other one, too?'

'No need,' I said. 'Did it hurt?'

'What?'

'When they took them away?'

'Dunno,' said Edmund. 'I was asleep. I mean, I was under. But it ached after. I was only six.'

I nodded. How in the world anyone had found out that he'd had twelve toes, if the eleventh and twelfth had been removed that long ago? He hadn't lived in the town for more than a year.

There was only one explanation. He must have told them himself.

At first I thought this was strange, but the longer I lay there thinking about it, the more unsure I became.

If I'd had twelve toes would I want to tell people about them? Maybe. Maybe not.

I didn't reach a conclusion and that bothered me. I don't know why.

Like almost every night that followed, we fell asleep to the sound of Henry's typewriter and to the sound of Henry's tape deck.

Elvis. The Shadows.

Buddy Holly, Little Richard, the Drifters.

And to the gentle scratching of tree branches against the window when the wind from the lake blew through the forest.

It felt good.

Almost too good, but then I was being selective. I was filtering out anything that wasn't within reach when we fell asleep at night or when we woke the next morning.

6

On our first few days at Gennesaret, we surveyed our kingdom. By sea and by land. Möckeln was four kilometres across, and that could be seen on the map. When rowing the boat, measures of distance felt pointless. Wherever you were going, it would take the time that it took; the important thing was to conserve your energy so you didn't wear your arms out before you got there. In the summertime, there was never any need to rush; time was an ocean one thousand times the size of Möckeln: you did as you pleased.

There were really only three destinations on the lake. Near the middle was Tallön, a barren islet only a couple hundred square metres in size where the seagulls liked to shit. Really there wasn't much there but bird shit, rocks and the ten knotted pines that grew in a circle in the centre, which had given the place its name. Well, the name it had on the map. Edmund and I called it Shit Island—or Seagull Shit Island: that rolled off the tongue better. With a normal wind it took one session to get there; by 'session' we meant that it was too short a trip to bother taking turns at the oars.

It took just about as long to get to Fläskhällen, a small beach with a cafe and twenty metres of sandy shore on the north end of the lake. From Gennesaret you could also take the gravel path through the woods, and it was much faster by bike than by boat.

The third destination for a boat trip was Laxman's supermarket in Åsbro. You expected it to take up half of an afternoon if you were doing the shopping—and of course you would be. If you were lucky, Britt would be in the shop. She was also a Laxman, was around our age, and known for being flighty. I wasn't sure what that meant; nor did I know how flightiness was expressed, but she had those glittering eyes and those plump lips and Edmund said he got a boner just thinking about her.

I didn't like it when Edmund discussed his feelings so plainly. Even if I unabashedly acknowledged that certain things also gave me an erection, it was a private matter. You didn't just talk about it willy-nilly. Eventually Edmund got the picture. Edmund was good at understanding awkward and sensitive things.

Whatever the case, we agreed that the hours it took to row to Laxman's and retrieve provisions were well spent. We drifted past the area crammed with summer cottages, and the jetties, keeping an eye out for girls of suitable size, even if there rarely were any, and then carried on to Mörk River. It was a lovely river. The reeds grew so tall and dense that in some places they were separated by only a metre-wide channel. It was better if you didn't meet a motorboat in this narrow, verdant passage— and Edmund and I both thought that our trips down this river could definitely be compared to a slow and steady infiltration of the Amazon's swampy jungle.

After a few days, we made an arrangement with Henry whereby we would be doing all the shopping, and as long as the summer lasted—before what happened happened—Edmund and I made the Mörk River journey every second or third day. We took turns rowing, of course. The one who was oarless rested on his belly in the bow of the boat and, with his senses on full alert, he kept an eye out for beaches and watched for the first sign of an approaching crocodile in the quaggy water.

Or a water snake. Or Indians.

Or he thought about Britt Laxman.

'*The Log Cabin on the Lingking River*,' said Edmund on one of our first expeditions. 'Have you read it?'

'No,' I said. 'I don't think so.'

'Damned good book. It reminds me of this. It's a grand summer, Erik. Shit, I hope it never ends.'

'Of course it won't,' I said. 'Toss me a liquorice stick.'

'Ay ay, Captain,' said Edmund. 'Do you think that Miss Laxman would be interested in a boat trip some time?'

'White man talk crazy,' I said. 'Laxman is really religious. I'm sure she's chained up behind the counter.'

'Hmm,' said Edmund. 'We'll have to take firearms and a metal saw next time. I can tell she'd be willing to satisfy a young man's every need.'

'With age come wisdom,' I said. This was a sign that I wanted to change the subject, and right on cue Edmund changed tack. As I said, he was perceptive. Uncommonly perceptive.

Between Gennesaret and the Sjölycke summer resort, there were two so-called real homesteads.

The first, the one that was closest to us, was a red shanty down by the edge of the lake, overgrown with reeds, alders, raspberry thickets and nettles.

And a lush broad-leaved forest, as my father would say with a knowing smile that I never fully understood.

When the house was in use, it was inhabited by one or more

members of the Lundin family, but it was often empty, because the male Lundins were usually locked up for something or other and the female Lundins were whores or nude dancers or madams and were more at home in an urban environment.

The most famous Lundin was Evert, who had stabbed a cop half to death when he was only a young boy, and later had moved on to bank robberies and arson, as well as racking up numerous assault charges. As far as I could tell, he preferred to assault women, but if there were none to hand, beating up pensioners or children would do. It was said that he was illiterate and never learned to tell left from right, no matter how hard he tried. This said a lot about the Lundin family.

You could say we shared a parking spot with the Lundins, because neither their house nor Gennesaret could be reached by car. Instead, there was a small clearing up the road where cars, bicycles or mopeds were parked. Then you had to walk along an uneven path for the last hundred metres. One hundred and fifty, if you wanted to get to the Lundins'. In the other direction, of course. There was a big difference between the Gennesaret path and the Lundin path.

Just as with the narrow and wide ways in the Bible, my mother had once explained.

But the Lundin path was both uneven and narrow, so it wasn't really a direct comparison. The other so-called homestead was an old soldier's cottage that lay on a bend past the winding gravel road that ran through the woods, set a good way up from the lake. The Levis lived there, an old Jewish couple who had survived Treblinka and who didn't interact with other people. Once a week, they rode down to the village on an old tandem bicycle with a cart that they loaded up at Laxman's with supplies for the next seven days.

At the time I didn't really know what it meant to have survived Treblinka, but I knew that it was too awful to talk about.

No one spoke of it, not my father, not my mother, or anyone else. It seemed as if it might've been better to have died in Treblinka than to have survived it. When I rode past the peaceful cottage in the woods, I thought that perhaps this is what the world was like. Some things were so bad you shouldn't even try to wrap your head around them. You had to just leave them be, preserving their invisibility and the silence enveloping them with the words you were forced to put to them.

The world, for all its good and evil, was far bigger than we knew, that I understood, and this fact made me feel both strangely calm and terrified.

I don't know why.

'What's the matter with your mum, really?' Edmund asked one afternoon after we'd cycled to Fläskhällen and bought ice cream. We sat by the grey picnic table above the sandy beach, which was empty because it was a cloudy day.

I bit the chocolate coating off my ice-cream bar before I answered.

'Cancer,' I said.

'Oh,' said Edmund, as if he understood. I don't think he did. Cancer was one of those words. Like Treblinka. Like death. Like fuck.

I didn't want to talk about them. Love? I wondered. Does that belong?

And as we sat there licking our ice cream and looking at the graffiti on the table—all the hearts and the Cock and Cunt and Bengt-Göran 22/7/1958—I chanted the words in my head, the whole ditty.

Cancer-Treblinka-Love-Fuck-Death.

I understood that all this existed in the world. Existed, existed, existed; and from then on—that whole summer—the chant came to mind occasionally, just those five words, like gibberish. No, not gibberish; more like a kind of incantation against something I understood, but didn't want to understand, I think.

Something shameful, perhaps, that the whole world—not just me—was also ashamed of. The plaster-language.

Especially when we cycled past the Levis, of course.

Cancer-Treblinka-Love-Fuck-Death.

I needed these words. Sometimes I wondered if it was a sign that I was going mad.

'Your brother Henry,' Edmund said one afternoon. 'What's he writing?'

'A book,' I said.

'A book?' said Edmund. 'Like *Introducing Rex Milligan*?'

It was part of the library of books he had brought with him. We'd both read it a few times already, and agreed that it was a real treat.

Introducing Rex Milligan by Anthony Buckeridge.

'No,' I said. 'It's something else, I think. Something serious.'

Edmund wrinkled his forehead and took off his glasses. He'd got them new for the summer and they were still in one piece, even though almost a whole week of holiday had already gone by.

'There's nothing wrong with being serious,' he said. 'I'd probably feel more at home in the world if people were a bit more serious.'

I'd never heard anyone our age say anything like that, not

even the boffins in our class, but when I thought about it, it actually made me happy.

'I guess I would, too,' I said.

It was also worrying.

'But seriousness shouldn't be taken too far,' said Edmund after a while. 'Then you'd sort of get stuck in it.'

'Like in a swamp,' I said.

'Exactly like in a swamp,' said Edmund.

And that was that.

During the first week out at Gennesaret the weather was varied, but mostly fine. The day we rowed to Seagull Shit Island and spoke in two-word sentences it was scorching, and we dived off the boat and from the island.

'Intolerable heat,' said Edmund.

'I agree,' I said.

'Fancy rowing?' said Edmund.

'Yes, please,' I said.

'Swim now,' Edmund said.

'Me, later,' I said.

The rules were simple. Every statement had to consist of two words: no more, no less. We alternated each line. If you wanted the other to be quiet, you kept quiet.

'Water cools,' I said.

'Only feet,' said Edmund.

We'd sat down in a crevice where the stones at our backs were slanted at an accommodating angle. Our legs dangled in the water. Picnic basket within reach. Transistor radio on. Dion, I think. And Lill-Babs singing 'Klas-Göran'.

'And legs,' I corrected him.

'Cools legs,' Edmund agreed.

'Yes, exactly,' I said.

'A sandwich?' asked Edmund.

'Not yet.'

'Thirsty, then?'

'Yes, please.'

'Cheers, brother.'

'Cheers, you.'

'Good life.'

'Yessir.'

'One word!'

'Two words!'

'Yes … sir?'

'Yes, naturally.'

'Not yessir?'

It was my turn and to mark that I was tired of splitting hairs, I kept quiet. After a while Edmund started to cough in such an exaggerated way that I was about to say 'Shut up!' but I managed to stop myself. Instead I sat a long while with my eyes closed facing the sun and controlled the silence between us.

I felt as though I had power over something I couldn't actually have power over. Words. Language.

It felt strange, too. Just as it did when you thought too hard about something.

'Your father?' I asked without opening my eyes.

'My father?' said Edmund.

'Has magazines?' I said.

'You mean?' said Edmund.

'Special magazines,' I elaborated.

Edmund sighed wearily.

'Special magazines,' he said.

I considered his tone.

'My apologies,' I said.

Edmund stretched one foot up to the sky and spread his toes. The delicate scar made a rare appearance.

'No need,' he said.

'Stomach rumbles,' I said.

'Mine, too,' said Edmund.

Henry came up and woke us on Saturday morning.

'I'm going to town,' he said. 'You'll be fine here; there's bangers and mash for dinner. I'll be late, so you'll have to fix it yourselves.'

'What are you going to do?' I asked.

Henry shrugged and lit a Lucky.

'Got a few things to take care of. By the way ...'

'Yes?'

'Are you going to Lackaparken tonight?'

'Perhaps,' I said. 'Why?'

Henry took a few drags and seemed to be thinking.

'We need a signal,' he said.

'A signal?' said Edmund.

Edmund didn't usually get involved when Henry and I were talking, and Henry looked at him with mock surprise.

'If I pull,' he said.

'Aha,' I said.

'Oh, right,' said Edmund.

'Listen,' said Henry after taking a couple more drags on the fag. 'If there's a tie around the flagpole, that means you go right up to bed if you come home later than I do. Okay?'

Edmund and I looked at each other.

'No objection,' said Edmund. 'A tie on the flagpole.'

'Right then,' said Henry and disappeared.

He left a swath of smoke and irritation behind him in the room. We lay there, waiting for it to disperse. We heard Henry slam the door downstairs and walk up the path.

'Your brother doesn't like me,' said Edmund after a few minutes.

I didn't know how to respond to that.

'Of course he does,' I said. 'Why wouldn't he?'

'It's fine,' said Edmund. 'You don't have to pretend.'

Cancer-Treblinka-Love-Fuck-Death, I thought. Why would I pretend?

'I don't know what you're talking about,' I said and went to sit on the loo.

7

We hung around for an hour down by the Sjölycke jetties the morning of that first Saturday, but it was mostly adults and kids splashing about and pissing in the water, so around noon we rowed out to Shit Island.

I had nicked six Lucky Strikes from some of Henry's many open packets, and we lay there surrounded by bird shit, drinking apple juice and smoking while we listened to *Sveriges bilradio*, a radio show for motorists, and the summer hit parade. It was as hot as ever and the skin on Edmund's back was already starting to peel. We played the two-word-sentence game, but soon tired of it, and then we didn't really talk about anything.

As I said, this wasn't a problem with Edmund. We reclined and smoked, sharing cigarette after cigarette and passing the bottles of juice between us. We were almost like an old married couple who had no need to say anything to each other at all.

No pressing need, anyway.

On the whole, it felt pretty good.

'Do you think about your life?' asked Edmund after we'd lain in silence for a few minutes listening to 'Young World' with our eyes closed in the sun, digging it, with the waves lapping at our calves. Edmund and I both thought that 'Young World' was a hit, no doubt, almost on par with 'Cotton Fields'.

'My life?' I said. 'How do you mean?'

'Well, what it's like,' said Edmund. 'If you compare it to others' lives, for example.'

'No,' I said. 'I guess I tend not to think about that.'

'If it could've been different somehow,' Edmund went on.

I waited before I said: 'You only have one life. The one you have. I don't see what good it would do to fantasize about anything else.'

Edmund drank some juice and scratched the bridge of his nose, as he did when he wasn't wearing his glasses.

'I mean, what if you had different parents?'

I didn't answer.

'How's your mum doing?'

'The cancer,' I said after a while. 'It is what it is.'

'Is she going to die?' said Edmund.

'No one knows,' I said.

'Us and our mums,' said Edmund and laughed.

'What do you mean?' I said.

'They're similar,' said Edmund. 'Yours has the cancer and mine has the bottle.'

'They're not at all alike,' I said. 'They're bloody different.'

I was irritated and Edmund noticed, because when he started talking again, he'd changed his tone.

'She's drying out this summer, my mum.'

I only vaguely knew what he meant.

'Drying out?'

'Vissingsberg,' said Edmund. 'The whole summer. She's going to learn to live without alcohol; she's done it several times already. That's why it's so good that I can be out here with you. Didn't you know?'

'No,' I said. 'But I don't see why it matters. If we're going to talk, let's talk about something else.'

'Okay,' said Edmund.

I knew he would have preferred to keep talking about his alcoholic mum, but I didn't fancy it. Instead we lay there and listened to the rest of the summer hit parade, smoked the last Lucky, and then we rowed back to Gennesaret to eat bangers and mash and to deck ourselves out for the night ahead.

We'd figured out that if we ate enough at home we wouldn't have to spend our cash on hot dogs in Lackaparken. So we ate the whole fifteen-pack of Sibylla; Edmund eight, me seven. And six portions of instant mash. I felt queasy afterward, but Edmund said he was on top form. We took a quick dip off the side of the boat—the floating dock wasn't yet finished and it was tricky getting in from the shore—bunged Brylcreem in our hair, pulled on clean nylon shirts and rode off on our bikes through the woods.

It wasn't more than five kilometres from Gennesaret to Lackaparken, but we took a few wrong turns and it was an hour before we arrived.

This early summer evening was like early summer evenings were at that time. Fragrant and rich with promise. Filled with nearly equal measures of lilac, jasmine and moonshine. At least around Lackaparken. We agreed that it was daft to spend three kronor on the entrance fee and parked our bikes a fair stretch into the woods. We made sure to chain them together, as well; it would be awful if some drunkard stole our bikes and we had to walk home in the middle of the night. You never knew.

Outside the entrance we bumped into Lasse Crook-mouth, whose parents had a cottage in Sjölycke. Crook-mouth was a bit older than we were, had left Stava School a few years back and his nickname came from his deformed head. Part of the lower half of his face was just sort of missing and when he spoke it looked as though he was trying to whisper into his own ear. I didn't know him particularly well. No one did; he usually kept to himself, whether that was because of his appearance or something else, I don't know.

'Mad Raffe is on duty,' he said, looking worried and even more deformed.

'Oh, bollocks,' I said.

When Mad Raffe was working it was hard to get in without paying. Here and there, you could force your way through the decaying wooden plank fence that surrounded the fairground—especially behind the stinking so-called 'conveniences' in the most densely wooded corner—but Mad Raffe was known for his ability to tell at a glance which visitors hadn't paid the entrance fee. Because this was probably his only talent, he made the most of it. He was especially intimidating and stubborn when he found an under-age kid who couldn't show him a valid ticket. Not to mention heavy-handed. That's why he was so often hired as a security guard; I could hardly imagine him taking payment for it, either. The uniform appeared to be payment enough. Whatever the case, there was no point in arguing with Mad Raffe; saying you had paid but lost the ticket was just about as futile as talking back to the police when you were caught riding your bike without lights.

'Are you going to pay?' wondered Lasse Crook-mouth.

Edmund and I dug into our pockets and counted our cash.

'I don't know,' I said. 'Are there any people in there?'

'Masses,' said Lasse Crook-mouth. 'Sod it. I'll chance it. Don't have any money anyway.'

Edmund and I arrived at a compromise. I would pay, and Edmund would hang back with Crook-mouth behind the urinals. Mad Raffe didn't really know who Edmund was because he was new in town, but he knew me more than well. He'd kicked both Benny and me out of Tajkon Filipson's World Famous Funfair at Hammarberg's field just under a month ago.

This logic proved to be sound. A half hour later, Mad Raffe came up to us three as we were messing about in front of the shooting gallery. Edmund slipped away and I triumphantly took out my yellow ticket and Lasse Crook-mouth was kicked out with a ruckus.

'You bloody shithead, you should have yourself committed!' he shouted when he was a safe distance down the road.

Mad Raffe just grinned and packed more dipping tobacco into his mouth. He rolled his yellow eyes, straightened his uniform and slipped into the crowd, on the hunt for new victims.

Duty above all.

I'd only visited Lackaparken twice before, both times the previous summer. There wasn't actually much for Edmund and me to do there. We weren't quite in the right age bracket to partake in the dancing, snogging and drinking.

But there was more on offer—flashes of what life would have in store in a few years. In addition to dancing and snogging, that is.

Like the poker tent. We made a beeline for it as soon as Lasse Crook-mouth was out of the picture. The smoky den was crowded with dozens of local talents trying to beat poker pro Harry Diamond and his wife Vicky Diamond. They were quite the attraction. You could feel the heat of their sins burning in your trousers as you neared the tent.

The game was a kind of stud poker; Harry played against three or four others at a time and Vicky dealt. She handled the deck as though she had been born with it in her hands, and it was impossible to tell if she was dealing from the top or the bottom. When the game was at a critical point, she'd lean so far forward that her burnished breasts threatened to spill from her dress, and then no one could keep their eyes on what she was doing with the cards. Everyone playing the game knew this trick, but it made no difference. Your eyes were drawn to her tits and you got taken for a ride, that's how it went.

This evening we watched Big Anton, Balthazar Lindblom's older brother, lose fifty kronor in less than fifteen minutes, and a fat egg-seller from Hjortkvarn storm out of the tent, promising to return to cut the bollocks off Harry and the baps off Vicky.

After the poker tent, we went to the arcade. There were only eight one-armed bandits under the sagging tarpaulin ceiling, but still we managed to lose our two kronor fairly quickly, and it was when we emerged from the tent, feeling pretty down, that we saw Ewa Kaludis.

She was standing by herself between the arcade tent and the dance floor, smoking a cigarette. Her dress was white, her bag hung nonchalantly on her shoulder—it was white as well—and I knew right away why she was alone in this sea of people.

She was simply too beautiful. Like a goddess or a Kim Novak. You can't fly too close to the sun, and everyone who saw her on that summer's eve knew it. The park had started to fall into shadow, particularly where the glow of the lanterns didn't quite reach, and Ewa Kaludis was standing in one of these darker spots. But the darkness made no difference; still, she sparkled—as if she were an angel or painted with one of those luminescent colours that Mr. Jonsson used to paint snowmen on the window of his toy shop for the Christmas display in December.

We stopped in our tracks, Edmund and I.

'Huh,' said Edmund.

I said nothing. I shut my eyes tightly and mustered the courage to walk up to her. The seconds felt like an eternity, and when I reached her, I felt much older.

'Hi, Ewa,' I said with more nerve than Colonel Darkin and Yuri Gagarin put together.

She lit up.

'Well, hello there,' she said smoothly. 'Fancy seeing you here.'

Her warm welcome rendered me speechless, but Edmund was only two steps behind and came to my rescue.

'Of course we are,' he answered. 'Has Madam been left to her own devices?'

I felt a strong pang of envy that I hadn't come up with that line myself. Masculine and protective yet cheeky.

She laughed and took a drag of her cigarette.

'I'm waiting for my fiancé,' she said.

'And where's he got to?' said Edmund.

She shrugged, and at that moment Berra Albertsson emerged from the dark together with Atle Eriksson, another handball player. They had their arms around each other's shoulders and were making a show of laughing at something. It was clear that they'd gone behind the tent for a piss and a drink. Berra let go of Atle and put his arm around Ewa Kaludis instead. And then he looked our way.

'And who are these babies?' he asked.

Atle Eriksson laughed so hard a mist of schnapps blasted from his mouth.

'Erik and Edmund,' said Ewa Kaludis. 'I got to know them at Stava. They're lovely boys.'

'I'm sure they are,' answered Super-Berra, pulling her closer to him. 'But now we're going to bloody well dance. Cheerio, you little shits!'

'Goodbye,' Edmund and I said in unison. And then they disappeared. We stood there, watching them go.

'What a prick,' said Edmund. 'I don't know what she sees in him.'

'Neither do I,' I said. 'Who knows what goes on in women's heads?'

'He makes you want to punch him in the face,' Edmund added.

'Exactly,' I said.

We wandered about Lackaparken for another few hours, noting that Britt Laxman clearly had something else on that night, and got rid of what little money we had as slowly as we could. Candy floss. The Chocolate Spin 'n' Win. A Loranga soda and a bloody expensive waffle with whipped cream and raspberry jam.

Just as we were about to make our way back to Gennesaret, we realized that we weren't the only ones that night who wanted to punch Super-Berra in the face.

On the whole, there hadn't been many fights, but the time had come: it was in the air. Edmund and I had just been behind the dance floor polishing off the last of the three Lucky Strikes I had pinched from Henry when we stumbled upon the whole gang.

Or rather, the gangs. Those who were going to fight and their right-hand men. On one side, Super-Berra, Atle Eriksson and a few staggering handball players. On the other, a cocky, red-faced man whom I'd never seen before. He was tattooed from head to toe and looked like a killer. And his corner men: half a dozen of just about the same kind.

'I'm going to give you what for, you fucking handball monkey!' slurred the red-faced one and tried to pull himself free from his corner men.

'Calm down, Mulle,' one of them insisted. 'Of course you can go a few rounds with that golliwog, but we have to lay low first ... the police, you know.'

Mulle nodded in a practised way. I didn't understand what he meant by 'golliwog'; Super-Berra did have dark, short-cropped hair, but he wasn't exactly black.

He was silent. He seemed calm and collected, and when everyone was shielded from view by the tent, he handed his striped blazer to one of the handball players, ceremoniously rolled up his sleeves and simply waited. Legs akimbo, with his guard up and wearing a crooked smile. His knees were slightly bent and he swayed, gently rocking from side to side, his hands loosely clenched. I realized that I was holding my breath and that Edmund was pressed up against me, grinding his teeth in anticipation. Other than the two gangs, Edmund and I were the only onlookers; the site of the bout had been carefully chosen, no doubt about it. I closed my eyes for a moment and took a deep breath. The night air was full of the smells of summer and schnapps. I wondered where Ewa Kaludis was now. 'Twilight Time' spilled from the dance floor, and it was getting late.

And then Mulle's companions released him. He let out an impressive roar—'Aaarrgh!'—tucked his head and charged at

Super-Berra. Even in the heat of the moment, I knew this was a terrible move. All Berra needed to do was step to one side— 'sidestep' as it's called in boxing—use the opponent's own momentum against him, and then knock him down.

And that's exactly what he did, but he didn't stop there. The florid Mulle bent double like a clubbed ox after that first punch, but then Berra lifted him up by the collar and gave him three or four more whacks before turning him around and bashing his head into the ground twice, with all his might.

My stomach lurched each time Mulle's head suffered a blow, and when it was done, I noticed a pall of silence had fallen over the fighters. Both Mulle's companions and the handball players were frozen and staring, and when Super-Berra straightened up and gestured for his blazer, Atle Eriksson handed it over without a word. Then they turned their backs on Mulle and walked away.

Solemnly. Like after a funeral. Edmund and I also slunk away. I felt ashamed for some reason and so did Edmund, I guess, because neither of us said anything until we'd left the park behind us and were unlocking our bikes.

'Christ, that was grim,' Edmund said and I thought I detected a slight tremble in his voice.

'And unfair,' I said. 'Bloody unfair. You don't hit a man when he's down.'

As we cycled back home through the woods, I thought about where Ewa Kaludis had been during the fight and if that was how you won over a woman like her.

By being like Berra Albertsson?

I remember that I shed silent tears as we trundled through the mild June night.

Yes, it was the middle of the night, the rear wheel of Edmund's bike chirred and I cried quietly without knowing why.

8

On Sunday, my dad came to visit. He didn't stay long because he'd got a lift from Ivar Bäck, who was supposed to help someone in Sjölycke with their TV antenna.

We sat outside on the lawn for an hour anyway and ate the watery strawberries that he'd brought with him and we talked. But not much. My mother was relatively well, my father said. She was going in for another series of tests. It would take a few weeks. Perhaps a month.

And then we'd see.

With age comes wisdom.

Henry offered to drive our father home in Killer when he went into town later that evening, but our father just shook his head.

'I'll go with Bäck,' he said. 'It's simplest that way.'

Afterward, Edmund asked what he meant by that. Why it was easier to go with Bäck.

I shrugged.

'He thinks Henry drives like a madman,' I said. 'He can barely stand being in a car with him.'

When my father was on his way, I noticed that he hadn't asked after Emmy Kaskel. Maybe Henry had told him after all.

'Mate,' said Edmund when he'd finished reading *Colonel Darkin and the Golden Ewes*. 'This is really something. You're going to be a millionaire.'

I'd finished *Colonel Darkin and the Golden Ewes* before we went out to Gennesaret, and I'd brought it with me, along with a new notebook. For a rainy day, or if the fancy struck.

The fancy struck, but it was impossible to keep the comic-drawing a secret from Edmund. After some deliberation, I'd left the notebook out with the other books half by chance, and it wasn't long until Edmund spotted it. And it wasn't much longer until he read it.

'It isn't any good,' I said. 'You don't need to pretend.'

'Not any good!' said Edmund. 'It's the best bloody thing I've seen since Nan got her tits caught in the mangler!'

This was a saying from Norrland and was meant to convey the highest praise and appreciation. I was suddenly so happy that I had a hard time hiding it.

'Oh,' I said. 'Sod off, you herring milt.'

This was another saying from Norrland.

My desire to draw certainly had something to do with what had happened on Saturday night at Lackaparken. I needed to draw and tell a story about a woman like Ewa Kaludis; the desire made me ache. Maybe I wanted to throw a few punches back—but in a cleaner way than in the fight between Super-Berra and Mulle. The day after, we'd started to discuss how Mulle might be feeling, but both Edmund and I got the chills when we thought about what his face must look like now. Not to mention how his head must be feeling.

In any case, there were a few rain showers on Sunday evening, and while Edmund was lying on his bed trying to write a letter to his mother in Vissingsberg, I drew the first panels of

Colonel Darkin and the Mysterious Heiress.

As the evening unfolded, I remember thinking how pleasant it was.

The more the summer progressed, the more my brother Henry was consumed with his existential novel. He was almost secretive about it. He often slept long into the day, got up and took a dip in the lake and sat down by the typewriter with coffee and a cigarette. Ideally out on the lawn by the wobbly garden table, weather permitting. Which it did, for the most part. When the question of supper arose, he almost always bowed out of kitchen duty and tossed Edmund and me five or ten kronor to take care of it: fetch provisions, cook and do the washing up.

It didn't bother us. Though money was tight, our basic needs were met, and it was nice to be able to buy an ice cream now and again. At Laxman's or by Fläskhällen. Or a few loose cigarettes; we couldn't always be nicking them from Henry, even if he would probably never have noticed.

After dinner Henry would disappear in Killer, and at least two out of three evenings Edmund and I were in bed before he returned. Sometimes I woke up in the middle of the night to the sound of the Facit's staccato clatter and the tape deck playing Eddie Cochran. The Drifters. Elvis Presley. He had recorded 'Wooden Heart' on several places on the tape. When the music ended, the birds singing in the bushes under the window took over. Sometimes I asked Henry how it was going with his book, but he never felt like talking about it.

'It's going,' he'd say and take a drag from his eternal Lucky.

It's going.

I was vaguely curious about what he was writing, but he never left any papers out and I didn't want to ask him more than once. One night, just after he'd driven away in Killer, I happened to catch sight of a sheet still in the machine on the desk. There were just a few lines on it; I cautiously sat down on the chair and turned the roller up a few notches so it would be easier to read.

I think I read the text five or six times. Maybe because I thought it was good, but also because it was so unexpected. Unexpected and eerie:

comes at him from behind, suddenly and immediately, stopping at just the right point. A step on the gravel, no more than one, hand tightly gripping the shaft, and then a brief fatal blow. When steel meets skull the sound that is born is mute. The reverse of a sound, audible because it is more silent than silence, and when the heavy body unites with the earth the summer night is dense and smiling enigmatically; everything slips into everything else and

He'd stopped there. I twisted the roller back, feeling like a thief in the night. As Benny's mother would say.

Cancer-Treblinka-Love-Fuck-Death, I thought. What sort of book are you writing, brother Henry?

It took a few days to plan our night raid on Karlesson's shop, and on Thursday, the day before Midsummer's Eve, we did the deed. Henry had apparently decided to stay home that night, but we said that we had something to do under the cover of night and soon after nine we were on our way. Henry didn't seem bothered.

'If you get up to no good, make sure you don't get caught,' he said without looking up from his typewriter.

We took four apple juices and a French loaf as provisions, and just over ten kronor, so we could each buy a sausage special at Törner's on the square before he closed at eleven.

At first all went as planned. It was a gusty night; a headwind was blowing over the plain, but we pulled into the square in Kumla at around quarter to eleven. Rain was in the air and there was barely a soul on the street. After we'd eaten our sausages and drained our apple juices, Törner sputtered home in his catering van and we started to look for spoons. When we'd finely combed the square we carried on to the rubbish bins outside Pressbyrån by the station and around the other sausage stand in town: Herman's by the tower block. By midnight we thought we had enough: fifty-three pieces. If you could expect about three balls and one plastic jobbie per go, it would all add up to one hundred and fifty balls and fifty-three jobbies.

But we couldn't possibly manage to chew all that gum and there probably wasn't more than that in Karlesson's dispenser anyway. We pedalled cautiously south along Mossbanegatan for the last two hundred metres. We didn't meet a soul. Not so much as a cat crossed our path. It began to drizzle. We could look forward to working undisturbed under the cover of night, no doubt about it. I buzzed with anticipation, and Edmund was giddy with excitement. We braked in front of the slumbering shop.

There were two handwritten notes on the empty glass container. On one it said 'Broken', on the other 'Not in serviss'. Karlesson wasn't known for his spelling.

I stared at the dispenser for a few seconds. Then I saw red. I wasn't normally one to lose the plot, but I couldn't contain my rage.

'Bloody fucking Cunt-Karlesson!' I screamed and then I

kicked the iron pole that the glass jar was mounted on with all my might.

I was only wearing flimsy blue plimsolls and the pain that shot up from the now broken toe was so intense that I thought I was going to faint.

'Calm down,' Edmund said. 'You'll wake the whole town, you nutter.'

I moaned and slid down the wall of the shop.

'Aw, hell, I think I broke a toe,' I whined. 'How the hell can the sodding dispenser be broken tonight of all nights? It hasn't been broken in three years.'

'Does it hurt?' Edmund wondered.

'Like the devil.' I forced the words through my clenched teeth.

But the first wave of bright white pain was already abating. I pulled off my shoe and tried to wiggle my toes. It didn't go well.

'God's finger,' said Edmund after watching my wiggling for a moment.

'What?' I said.

'The fact that the dispenser is kaput,' said Edmund. 'It must mean that we weren't supposed to raid it tonight. It wasn't meant to be, you know. God's finger. That's what it's called.'

I had a hard time being interested in anyone's finger with my toe hurting so much, but I suspected that Edmund had a point.

'Is there another dispenser in town?' he asked.

I thought about it.

'Not outside. They have one inside Svea's, I think.'

'Hmm,' said Edmund. 'What should we do?'

I tried to put my shoe back on. I couldn't, so I shoved it in my rucksack and opened an apple juice instead. Edmund sank down next to me and we each took a sip.

And then the police car arrived.

The black-and-white Amazon came to a halt right in front of us and the driver rolled down the window.

'What are you two doing?'

I was speechless, even more speechless than when I'd stood before Ewa Kaludis in Lackaparken. More speechless than a dead herring. Edmund got up.

'My friend hurt his foot,' he said. 'We're on our way home.'

'Is it serious?' asked the police.

'No, we'll be fine,' said Edmund.

'You can have a lift if you need one.'

'Cheers,' said Edmund. 'Maybe another time.'

I stood up to show that everything was indeed fine.

'All right,' said the police. 'Get on home now, it's late.'

And then they drove away. We hung back until their red taillights were out of sight. Then, Edmund said: 'See? God works in mysterious ways. Now tell me, is there another dispenser in Hallsberg?'

We made off with 166 balls, 45 rings and 20-something other invaluable plastic thingies from the chewing-gum dispenser by the train station kiosk at Hallsberg. It went smoothly; the clock on the station building read five past two when we were done and my toe didn't hurt at all any more. It was stiff and swollen and numb, but what did that bloody matter when you had a week's worth of gum?

Edmund didn't try to conquer Kleva that night. Instead, we walked all the way up the hill, which took quite a long time because of my broken toe. Over the next few days, I'd learn that it was much easier to cycle than to go on foot.

During the last stretch, from Åsbro and through the forest, rain began to pour, and by the time we tossed our bikes aside up by the parking space, we were exhausted. In addition to Killer and a few of the Lundins' old motorbikes, a moped was parked there. A red Puch. If I hadn't been so wet and tired, I might've recognized it.

When we reached the house, the rain stopped. The sun was on its way up and one of Henry's ties was knotted around the flagpole.

9

On the afternoon of Midsummer's Eve, both of our dads came out to visit for a few hours. Mr. Wester was on top summer form; in addition to herring and new potatoes he brought a bundle of blue and yellow paper flags and an accordion. The weather was quite nice; we ate at the table out on the lawn while he serenaded us. 'The Rush of the Avesta Rapids', 'Afternoon at Möljaren' and a couple more I didn't recognize. As well as one of his own songs called 'For Signe'.

As he played it, tears welled in his eyes, and I noticed that there weren't any women around. 'We're out', as Karlesson said when you wanted something he didn't have in stock.

Five men celebrating Midsummer as best they could, and I tried to play a little time travel game with myself. What would it be like in ten years? Would my father and Edmund's father be all alone then? Would Henry have settled down and had a family? And Edmund? It was hard to imagine Edmund with a wife and children. Four wee Edmunds with broken glasses and six toes on each foot.

And what about me?

'It's tragic,' said Edmund's dad and put the accordion aside. 'As with life, so with summer. It's only just begun and suddenly it's autumn. Tragic.'

But then he laughed out loud and helped himself to more herring and potatoes.

'Truer words were never spoken,' said my father.

Henry sighed and lit a Lucky Strike.

They left us around five, our fathers; they'd only borrowed their colleague's car for the afternoon and were both working the evening shift at the prison. Edmund's dad suggested that they pick nine different types of flowers to place under their pillows, but my father wasn't particularly amused by the idea.

'We already know which women we'll be dreaming of,' he said with a half-hearted smile. Then they waved farewell and walked up to the clearing where they'd parked the car.

Edmund and I had decided to check out Fläskhällen, where they usually celebrated Midsummer by raising a maypole, dancing and the whole kit and caboodle. He'd be damned, Edmund said, if Britt Laxman didn't turn up at a place like that, and as soon as we were done with the washing up we climbed in the boat and rowed away. When we were out on the lake, Edmund said: 'Were you awake at all last night?'

'Awake?' I said. 'What do you mean?'

'Well, maybe you heard something.'

'Heard what?'

Edmund stopped rowing.

'Your brother, of course. And that bird, whoever she is. They were going at it.'

'I see,' I said and tried to sound disinterested. 'No, I was sleeping like a log.'

Edmund looked at me hesitantly and we didn't speak for a while.

'Shall we switch places?' I asked when we'd gone about half-way.

'No, no,' said Edmund. 'You need to rest your toe.'

'My toe isn't going to be doing the rowing,' I said.

But Edmund didn't relinquish the oars and we neared the music from Fläskhällen, I rested on the stern thwart, running my hand through the water, trying to not think about what'd gone on during the night.

Or the morning, rather. We hadn't gone to bed until after three and then not a sound had come from Henry's room.

I couldn't really get my thoughts in order; while it was certainly arousing to know that my brother might've been having sex with a girl right beneath our floorboards, it was scandalous somehow, too. As if Edmund had unearthed a shocking family secret. As if I should feel ashamed of what Henry was up to. Of course it was bloody useless to think along these lines, I'd be the first to admit that. If there was one thing in this world I envied it was the ability to find yourself a girl and get it on. That was sort of what life was all about, wasn't it?

I slipped my whole arm into the water. I tried as hard as I could to think about something else, but it didn't work, like I said. Edmund rowed along, carefree, and didn't seem to be trying to think of anything else. Quite the opposite.

'This is a brilliant summer, Erik,' he said as we approached the channel of reeds. 'In every way. It's probably the best I've had.'

I was struck by how much I liked Edmund. There were two weeks left until the Incident, my mother lay dying of cancer, I had broken a toe, but yes, it was indeed a brilliant summer in every way.

So far.

Neither Edmund nor I thought that Midsummer at Fläskhäl-len was in any way a brilliant affair. Sure, Britt Laxman may have been the first person we caught sight of when we pulled up in the boat, but she was clearly being escorted by a red-haired bloke wearing sunglasses and winklepickers, and we could tell that we weren't going to get much joy there. A few drunken lads in sporting kit were sitting around drinking coffee spiked with moonshine. A three-man band was taking a breather when we arrived, and they really should have spent the rest of the night on a break—an accordion, a guitar and a double bass that seemed to be strung with old rubber bands. Four couples pretended to dance, some with clogs, some without, some with the music, some without, and a few scattered groups of people around our age messed about listlessly trying to look like President or Mrs. Kennedy. We played a round of golf and tried to get off with two giggling Jacqueline-alikes from Skåne, but they soon retreated to their families' caravans, which were lined up over in the camping area.

The campsite wasn't exactly large, but it was by no means full: four caravans, as many sagging tents and a half-dozen cows who either had got lost or had been brought there as lawnmowers by the farmer, Grundberg, who also ran the businesses at Fläskhällen beach.

Inside the cafe was a new pinball machine. It was called a Rocket 2000; we tried our best to have a go, but a gang of youths from Askersund who had arrived on mopeds seemed to have a flood of one-krona coins to pour into the machine. In the end we decided to postpone the game. Soon after we saw that Britt Laxman and the red-haired boy were sitting down by the fire on the beach, grilling sausages on the same stick, so we gave up and rowed back to Gennesaret.

My father had taught me that there's no point being stubborn when the odds are against you, and Edmund agreed wholeheartedly.

'When the going gets tough, the tough get going, you bastard son of a mosquito-slag,' he'd said. He'd told me that was the kind of thing you said man-to-man deep in the forests of Hälsingland, and I had no reason not to believe him.

When we were out on the water, Edmund confided in me. He started with a question.

'Have you ever been beaten up? I mean really beaten up.'

I didn't think so, I said. I'd never been given more than a slap or a horse-bite pinch or an accidental blow to the solar plexus. Or a few whacks with Benny's hockey stick after I sat on it and broke it by accident.

'I have,' Edmund said gravely. 'When I was little. By my dad. Lots of bloody times.'

'Your dad? What are you talking about? Why would your dad—?'

'Not him,' Edmund interrupted. 'The other one, my real dad. Albin is just my stepdad; he married Mum when my real dad disappeared. Cor, how he let rip … on Mum and me. Once he hit Mum so hard she lost her hearing.'

'Why?' I asked. I didn't know what else to say.

Edmund shrugged.

'He was like that.' He thought for a moment. 'You never forget. How it feels. How … how scared you get, lying there, waiting. Waiting is almost worse than the beating itself.'

'I understand,' I said. 'Is that why your mum is an alcoholic?'

'I think so,' said Edmund and dipped his glasses in the water to rinse them clean. 'He drank like there was no tomorrow, and taught her how … but she was born with a pedigree. Grandpa drank enough for an entire platoon.'

'Where is he now, your real dad?'

'No idea,' said Edmund. 'He disappeared when I was five and a half; Mum refuses to talk about him. Albin came into the picture quite soon after.'

I nodded.

'Violent people are bloody awful,' said Edmund as he put his dripping glasses back on. 'I can't stand people who prey on the weak.'

'It is bloody awful,' I agreed. 'You shouldn't have to stand for it.'

Henry was gone by the time we got back and we spent the rest of the night playing Chinese chequers and chewing gum. We came up with our own variation where we played using balls of chewing gum. There was something about chewing your opponent's gum if you jumped over it, but we never quite settled on the rules. We went to bed early; we hadn't slept much the night before, especially Edmund, and we couldn't care less about putting flowers under our pillows and all that romantic nonsense.

I drew a few panels of my comic before I fell asleep, and Edmund wrote a letter to his mother at Vissingsberg. He hadn't been happy with his previous attempts, and now he was trying a lighter, more masculine approach. When he was finished, he tore the page right out of his notebook and handed it to me.

'What do you think?' he said chewing his pen.

It read:

Mornin', Mum!

*I'm having a gay old time out here. I hope you're sober and
are as happy as a clam. See you in the autumn.*
  Your one and only Edmund

'It's great,' I said. 'She's going to frame it and hang it over her
bed.'

'I think so, too,' said Edmund.

Not a single sound came from the downstairs that night,
not even from the tape deck, but at some point toward the
morning I woke to the sound of firecrackers being shot off and
rockets being launched over at the Lundins'. Apparently, they
were having some sort of family gathering; we hadn't heard a
peep from them for two weeks, but it was just like them to an-
nounce themselves in this way. And on Midsummer's Eve, too.

Anyway, I soon fell asleep again, and then I had a strange
dream about Henry getting his tie caught in his typewriter.
He was frantically pounding on the keys trying to get free, but
with each line the tie was pulled tighter. In the end—when his
nose was practically on the roller—he called for help. Well, it
was more of a hiss because he could barely breathe. I cut off
the tie, and as thanks he hit me and explained that it was a
bloody expensive tie and I had ruined an entire chapter.

Even as I was dreaming, I thought it was strange, and when
I woke up I was still mad at Henry. It was rotten of him to hit
me after I'd saved his life. It didn't matter if it was a dream or
reality: it was unfair.

But when I got up, he was already sitting on the lawn, writing and smoking. In just his pants and without any sign of a
tie; it must have just been one of those dreams that had got

out of hand. Meaningless, no matter how you twisted it and turned it around. I went out to him.

'How's it going?' I asked. 'With the book.'

He leaned back and squinted at the sun, which had just broken through the clouds.

'Rolling along,' he said. 'It's rolling along, little brother.'

And then he laughed that short, sharp laugh of his and went on clattering.

I hesitated before I asked, 'Did you find yourself a new girl?'

He typed until it pinged at the end of the line.

'I'm working on it,' he said and looked thoughtful. 'Yes, I am. There's a lot I'm working on.'

I couldn't figure out what he meant, so I asked.

'It means everything,' said my brother, and then he laughed again. 'Everything.'

10

During the last week of June it was so hot, the bog was boiling.

At least it felt that way if you forgot to cover it properly with peat moss litter, and there was a clear advantage to holding in your shit until the evening.

The need to periodically cool off in the lake became much more pressing—as well as the need to finish the floating dock. It was too much of a faff to go out in the boat every time you wanted to take a dip, and none of us—neither I nor Edmund nor Henry—was especially fond of teetering around on the sticky bottom where you might sink down to your knees in a mud hole or trip on a root and land on your face.

So, the dock. It was about time. We'd already transported six empty barrels from Laxman's and Henry had sketched it out. Hammers, ropes, nails and saws were stored in the shed by the privy. Wood was the only thing missing.

Planks.

'The Lundins,' said Henry when the sun was high in the sky of a new day, hotter than Marilyn Monroe's kisses. 'You're going to have to nick a few planks from the Lundins' pile.'

'Us?' I said.

'You,' said Henry. 'I've got a lot to do. You want to have a dock, don't you?'

'Yes, we do,' I said.

'All right, then,' said Henry. He put on the old straw hat that he'd bought at a flea market in Beirut and went to his typewriter in the shade. 'Twenty kronor if you're done before nightfall!' he called out when he'd sat down. 'Shouldn't be a problem for two sharpshooters such as yourselves.'

'Who says it's a problem?' said Edmund. 'What a load of rubbish.'

But he said it quietly, certain that Henry couldn't hear.

The Lundins' timber stockpile lay next to the path down to their house, not more than ten metres from the parking spot up by the road. It was a considerable pile, hidden by an old, mouldy tarpaulin, and it had lain there as long as I could remember. Most likely some of them had nicked it from a building site a long time ago and couldn't be bothered to carry it any further than just out of sight from the road—and most likely none of them would care in the slightest if a few planks went missing from the pile.

Especially if they didn't notice.

The safest thing would have been to launch our mission under the cover of night. But you never really knew with the Lundins. They had their own circadian rhythm. It was also clear that at least a few of them had arrived for the summer now; we'd heard a bit of a commotion over the past days: swear words, glass breaking, and so on.

Another reason not to go at night was of course that twenty kronor were on the line, so we really just had to pull ourselves up by the bootstraps and get on with it. No hesitation, no objections: Edmund and I agreed on that point.

You could say that our mission was a success. For a few hours, we dragged planks through the marshy, inhospitable midge and gadfly hell that lay between the Lundins and Gennesaret. We swore and were stuck with thorns, swore and were bitten, swore and made our way down, scratching ourselves up and bruising our bodies all over. The heat drove us mad, but we did it. We made it.

By twelve thirty we had amassed a respectable pile of planks that Henry—leaning back, lifting his hat, squinting and lighting a Lucky Strike—deemed sufficient.

'Good, good,' he said. 'Do you need a hand? It'll cut into your fee, obviously.'

'Like hell we do,' we said.

While we sawed and hammered and fastened we talked about Edmund's real dad. And about why he was so violent. Because it seemed strange—at least to me.

'He was sick,' said Edmund. 'He had an unusual brain disorder. When he drank, he got aggressive.'

'Sustained,' I said. 'Why did he drink?'

'That was another part of the illness,' Edmund suggested. 'He simply had to have alcohol. Or else he'd go mad. Yes, that's how it was …'

'So, either he went mad or he went mad?' I said.

'Exactly,' said Edmund. 'That's how it is for some people. It's a shame that it had to be my dad.'

'Bloody depressing,' I said. 'He shouldn't have been a dad at all.'

Edmund nodded.

'But it wasn't like that in the beginning. Before I was born. The illness came creeping … then it was what it was.'

'Hmm,' I said. 'Is it hereditary?'

'Don't know.'

A few seconds passed.

'But I hate him anyway,' Edmund said with rising anger. 'It's so damn cowardly to attack people who can't defend themselves. And with a belt … Why did he have to use a belt, can you tell me that?'

I couldn't.

'Hitting a person when they're down—'

He broke off. I pictured Mulle's ruddy, unconscious face, and recalled how Super-Berra had lifted it up and bashed it into the ground.

'Mm,' I said. 'There's nothing worse. Do you think you'll look him up when you get older? Your real dad. Track him down and corner him?'

'Yessir,' said Edmund. 'You can count on it. For that reason alone I hope that he's still alive. I have it all worked out. First I'm going to find him and not tell him who I am, and then I'm going to be nice to him, sweeter than honey, buy him a coffee and some cake … and a drink … and then when he least expects it I'll tell him who I am and then I'll lay into him so hard that he'll hit the ground. And then—'

And that's when Edmund hit his thumb with the hammer and started swearing and screaming blue murder. I never found out how he was going to continue exacting revenge on his father. What would I have done in his shoes? Would I have felt the same way? I couldn't work it out.

So, I decided that I didn't want to think about the situation at all. One more. Cancer-Treblinka-Love-Fuck-Death.

And Edmund's dad.

I slotted him in between Fuck and Death. Preliminarily.

Even though it was hot, I liked sawing and nailing and building. Especially nailing. When you hammered nails, it was as if you didn't need to think about the things that you didn't want to be thinking about. You could just concentrate on what you were doing. Bang. You just had to bang on. Drive the nail into the wood. Bang. Bang that bugger. Bang. Bang. Bang. And then that extra bang when it was in its place. When it couldn't go in any further.

Bang. To put it in its place. Now you're in there, you wretched nail, and that was the idea all along. Even if you tried to be stiff and crooked and worm your way left and right. You shitty nail. I'm the one in charge here. Damn right. I thought of our teacher Gustav in school and saw that there was woodwork and then there was woodwork.

The sun was still high when we were done. Henry inspected the eight-metre-long building project, checking to see if the barrels were secured properly. He said was going to make pancakes while we put the dock in place.

'Okay?'

'Sure,' said Edmund and we started to drag the fruit of our labour to the edge of the lake. Following Henry's drawing, we moored the dock with four ropes to two stable birches and anchored it with a half-slack hawser both at the end of the dock and closest to the shore. A bit of slack was necessary, Henry had explained, but not too much. Then we stood and admired the wonder for a while before we strode out over the planks. It was a bit wobbly and here and there your feet sank below the water line, at least when there were two of you, but, yes, it worked. We had built a bloody dock.

Now we had a floating dock and twenty kronor. We looked at each other with satisfaction.

'A brilliant summer,' said Edmund with a slight tremble in his voice. 'Huzzah, as they said in Ångermanland.'

At the far end of the dock the water was nearly two metres deep and we managed to dive off thirty-eight times before Henry came out and shouted that the pancakes were ready. We ate as if we'd never seen food before and then went out and dived into the lake thirty-eight more times. We thought the sun might never set that night, so after Henry had made his debut dive and paid us our promised ten kronor each, we lay on the dock, reading or playing cards, which was tricky. You had to keep your arse in the wagon—as Edmund said in his Norrlandish way—otherwise the cards got wet.

But never mind. The point was that we were lying on the planks that we'd swiped and hammered together ourselves. And floating on barrels we'd transported ourselves all the way from Laxman's and had expertly bound together. That was what this never-ending hot day was all about. Lying on your own dock.

'King of spades,' said Edmund. 'I hear a moped.'

I listened. Yes, the sharp noise of a moped zipping along was coming from the forest. It seemed to be just about level with the Levis'.

'Yes,' I said. 'Pass. A Puch, I think.'

We had played another few hands before we heard it stop and switch off up by the parking area. That made us lose our concentration. If we'd had any to lose in the first place.

'Eh,' said Edmund. 'I'm tired of this game. Let's call it a day.'

'Works for me,' I said, collecting the cards. I sat up on the dock with my legs in the water and looked toward the edge of the woods. Henry walked out on to the lawn and I noticed that he had put on jeans and a white nylon shirt.

I don't know if I had time to sense what was coming—afterward, Edmund claimed that he had anyway—but just over a minute after the moped's engine had been turned off up by the road, Ewa Kaludis appeared on Gennesaret's lawn. She wore a short white dress and a red shirt over it; when she spotted Henry she laughed and pulled a bottle of wine out of her tote bag—then she pressed herself against him and his white shirt.

Right then Edmund started to hiccup, an affliction that would last for several hours.

'No fucking way, hiccup,' he said. 'Your brother and Ewa Kaludis. Then it was them, hiccup, I heard … no fucking way.'

I got up, lost my footing, almost fell into the water, and then made my way to the shore. Henry and Ewa Kaludis turned toward me. Edmund hiccupped again. I felt paralyzed—as if I had lost all sensation in my legs and had no choice but to stand here on this patch of grass and earth for the rest of my life. In a dripping, faded bathing suit—Oh well, it'd dry eventually … I swallowed and closed my eyes and counted to one, then Henry said: 'So, Erik. Brother. There's a lot I'm working on, like I said. A lot.'

'Hi, Erik,' said Ewa Kaludis. 'And hello, Edmund.'

'Hi, hiccup,' said Edmund from behind me. He sounded like a frog down by the edge of the lake. I opened my eyes and got my tongue and legs going again.

'Hi there, Miss Kaludis,' I said. 'I was just going to the bog. See ya.'

I sat there a while. Reading the same page of True Stories in an old issue of *Reader's Digest* fifty times. I don't know what was buzzing more—the three-quarters-full, summer-warmed drum of shit beneath me or my fried noodle of a head—but I sat where I sat and it took a while. Only when Edmund knocked on the door and wondered if I'd had a shit-thrombosis—a rare illness from the depths of Medelpad—I pulled on my swimming costume and gave up. I opened the door and stepped out into the world.

'Hiccup,' said Edmund and tried to smile like Paul Drake. 'What do you think about Berra Albertsson … and everything.'

'I don't know,' I said.

'Some brother you have there,' said Edmund, but it was clear that he was more worried than he was letting on.

'He's out of his mind,' I said.

'Hiccup,' said Edmund. 'You smell like shit.'

Cancer-Treblinka … I started to think, but I had already forgotten where Edmund's father went.

'Maybe we should just have a swim?' I said.

'You're preaching to the converted,' said Edmund.

We swam until the sun had fully set and the midges started to buzz like mad at the edge of the shore. Ewa Kaludis and Henry were on the dock, testing it out, and Ewa said that it seemed to be a sterling dock.

A sterling dock. I floated on my back out in the water and my entire body blushed. And wondered what would happen tonight.

'Exactly,' said Edmund and sprayed water like a seal. 'Built to last, hiccup. No more, no less.'

Ewa Kaludis laughed.

'You're a funny one, Edmund,' she said.

Then she linked arms with Henry and they started to walk back toward the house.

My brother Henry and Ewa Kaludis. She hadn't swum all

day, even though it had been so warm. Who knew why? Maybe she didn't have a swimming costume with her.

But she did try out the dock. Sterling work.

11

Before my mother got sick with cancer she said a number of strange things. It was in the weeks right before the diagnosis; maybe she sensed misfortune coming and wanted to make sure she had imparted some of her wisdom. A few words for the road before it was too late, I suppose.

'You're the dove, Erik,' she would say, looking at me with her mild, watery eyes. 'Henry is the hawk; he always manages to come out on top. But you, you we have to be careful with, you're the one who has to watch his step.'

Those exact words came to mind when it started to sink in that Henry was involved with Ewa Kaludis. That he was actually *with* her. I mulled over the idea of the dove and the hawk and, thinking of Berra Albertsson, reflected on how lucky it was for Henry that he was a bird of prey. Because when Super-Berra found out what was going on between Ewa and my brother, well, there were sure to be consequences. That was my view, at least, but I knew what a miserable amateur I was when it came to navigating love's labyrinths.

And Edmund wasn't any more skilled. Not at all.

Love is like a train, I'd heard Benny's mum say once. It comes and goes. Maybe there was something to it, but Benny's mother was no expert in matters of the heart.

But I didn't really think about it; you couldn't quite put

words to it. My brother and Ewa Kaludis. Kim Novak on the red Puch. Her breast against my shoulder in the classroom. Berra Albertsson and red-faced Mulle in Lackaparken.

That was more than enough already.

Anyway, we didn't hear much that night. Nothing that suggested that they were lying there, doing it. They had the tape deck on low; Ewa laughed now and again: it had a sort of cooing sound. Henry's hoarse guffaw rose through the floorboards a few times, too. That's it. Maybe they were just sitting and talking: what did I know? That might be what you did sometimes. When you weren't in the mood.

Still, Edmund and I stayed awake in the dark. We lay completely still in our beds and pretended to be sleeping until we heard Ewa and Henry say goodbye out on the lawn. A minute passed and then the Puch fired up in the clearing. Edmund sighed deeply and turned toward the wall. I looked at my self-illuminating watch. It was half two; it had probably started to get light outside, but we had the blinds pulled down as usual.

Cancer-Treblinka-Love-Fuck-Death, I thought despondently.

And Edmund's dad. And Henry and Ewa Kaludis. No, that was too heavy, as I said. Not worth thinking about.

It was nothing for a fragile dove to trouble his fried-noodle head with.

'It's a sensitive situation, you understand. Sensitive.'

Henry looking earnestly at us across the dining table. First me, then Edmund. We looked back at him equally earnestly and each swallowed a lump of macaroni. It's much easier to appear earnest and to inspire confidence when your gob isn't stuffed with macaroni. Especially if you happened to have mixed in too much flour, as Edmund had done this time.

'Of course,' I said.

'Discretion is the better part of valour,' said Edmund.

I had no idea what that meant, but Edmund was full of strange expressions:

Discretion is the better part of valour.

Something is rotten in the state of Denmark.

Seh la gehr, *as the Germans say.*

Not to mention all the Norrlandish.

'Good,' said Henry. 'I trust you. But remember that even if you think you know a lot, there's very little that you understand.

'That doesn't just go for you. It applies to me too,' he added after a while. 'And to everyone else.' He waved his fork in the air in front of him, as if he wanted to write what he was saying on the air. 'We would do much better, we people, if we stopped creating bloody context all the time. We should be living in the moment.'

He fell silent and lit a Lucky Strike. Pensively blowing smoke across the dining table. It wasn't often that Henry let more than one sentence slip at a time, at least not with us, and the effort seemed to have tired him out.

'In the moment,' said Edmund. 'I've always thought so.'

'How's the book coming?' I quickly asked.

'What?' said Henry, staring at Edmund.

'The book,' I said. 'Your book.'

Henry took his eyes off Edmund and took a drag.

'Wonderfully,' he said and stretched his arms over his head. 'But you're not allowed to read it until you've turned twenty, remember that.'

'Why not?'

'Because it's that kind of book,' said my brother Henry.

The hawk protecting the dove, I thought, and then that half-page came to mind. The one I'd read eight or ten days ago, about the body that landed on the gravel road and the dense summer night. Suddenly I felt ashamed: as if without warning I had found myself in possession of something that was apparently forbidden and inappropriate for children. I muttered something vague in reply, but it seemed a response wasn't actually necessary, so I hastily shovelled more macaroni in my mouth.

'I was thinking about visiting Mum tomorrow,' said Henry when he'd stubbed out his cigarette. 'Want to tag along?'

I finished chewing again.

'No thanks,' I said. 'I don't think so. In a week or so, maybe.'

'As you wish,' said Henry.

'Say hello for me,' I said.

'Of course,' said Henry.

'The soul is located just behind the vocal cords.' That was another one of those strange things my mother said before she was admitted to hospital. 'If you listen carefully, you'll always be able to tell the difference between right and wrong. Remember that, Erik.'

The day after E-Day (E as in Ewa Kaludis) we rowed through the creek to get provisions from Laxman's, and I asked Edmund where he thought the soul lived in the body. And about right and wrong.

It didn't seem as if Edmund had ever thought about it, because he missed a stroke and we glided right into the reeds. It was easily done, really: the creek seemed to be getting narrower and narrower with each passing day; the cottage owners usually got together and cleared it out once every summer, but it hadn't happened yet this year.

'Your mum has a handle on right and wrong,' said Edmund when we had got ourselves back on course. 'Of course you know when you're doing something bad. When you're mean to someone or whatever …'

'Or you've ripped off a gum dispenser?' I said.

Edmund mulled that over for a moment.

'Chewing gum is one of the ills of youth, I'm sure of it. So, ripping off a gum dispenser can never be completely wrong,' he said.

'But it must be a bit wrong?' I suggested. 'As is stealing planks.'

'Hardly,' said Edmund. 'It's peanuts compared with … well, if you compare it.'

He looked solemn, and I understood what he was comparing it to. Neither of us said anything for a while, but then he feathered the blades of the oars, placed them on the gunwales of the boat and started to grab at his body.

'But where the soul is, devil knows. I think it moves around. When I eat, it's in my stomach. When I read, it's in my head. When I think about Britt Laxman—'

'Enough,' I interrupted. 'I get it. You have a nomadic soul; that's probably because you've spent so much of your life moving around.'

'Maybe,' said Edmund, taking hold of the oars again. 'Have you told your brother about the fight in Lackaparken, how it escalated?'

'No,' I said. 'Why do you ask?'

'Because my gypsy-soul tells me that it would be right to let him know.'

I sat in silence for a few seconds.

'Henry always comes out on top,' I said. 'He's been to sea twice.'

'Well, then,' said Edmund. 'I was just thinking. Damn, it's hot.'

'Long, hot summer,' I said.

'That's a cracking song,' said Edmund. 'It can't hurt for us to be on the alert, both you and me. About Henry and Ewa and what they're up to. What do you think?'

'White man speak with forked tongue,' I said.

It was one of the best lines I knew. It could be used in any situation, except when you were talking to a Red Indian, and Edmund didn't have anything to add.

'No further questions,' is all he said and continued rowing along the channel of reeds.

A few nights later I woke when Edmund sat up in his bed, panting.

'What's the matter with you?' I asked.

'He must have picked her up in the car,' said Edmund. 'In Killer. I didn't hear a moped.'

'What are you on about?'

'Listen,' said Edmund and now I heard it, too.

Two distinct sounds.

One was Henry's bed creaking and groaning. Rhythmically and calmly. The other was Ewa Kaludis whining. Or moaning. Or gurgling. I didn't know which because I'd never heard a woman make noises like that before.

'My, my, my,' whispered Edmund. 'They're going at it so hard the whole house is shaking. I think I'm going to blow.'

His childish nonsense upset me.

'Shut up, Edmund,' I said. 'You shouldn't talk about it like that.'

Edmund fell silent. Leaving only the sound of Henry's bed, rhythmically, insistently reverberating through the night. Throughout the house.

'Sorry,' said Edmund after a while. 'You're right, of course. But I'm going to sneak down and check it out anyway.'

'Check it out?' I said.

'Sure,' said Edmund. 'We can spy on them from the stairs. They don't have a blind down there. It'll be educational. Come on, don't hang about.'

For the first time in my fourteen-year-old life I had an erection that was so hard it hurt.

Edmund had probably thought we could each sit on a step and eyeball them, but that didn't work. The ramshackle stairs ran up to our room along the gable wall, but were a bit above the window in Henry's room. If we were going to see anything, we'd have to stand in the flower bed near the wall with peonies, mignonettes and a hundred different types of weeds. As stealthily as Indians, we sneaked there, and twice as stealthily as Indians we popped our heads up above the window ledge.

And then we saw everything.

It was like a film, but there weren't any films like that at that time, way back at the start of the sixties. But I had the vague notion that they'd exist in twenty years' time. Or thirty. Or a hundred; never mind, at some point there'd be films like this, if only for the simple reason that they were necessary.

I had that vague notion. The rest wasn't so vague.

Ewa Kaludis was sitting astride my brother. She was naked and her breasts were dancing as she moved up and down on top of him. They were partly turned in our direction—well, she was, and that was the main thing. They'd lit a few candles in empty bottles; the flames flickered every now and then and cast patterns of shadows on her body.

Across her bare face and bare shoulders and bare breasts. Her slender, curvy, shining belly heaving and rolling and the glimpses of her dark sex, which was sometimes hidden by one of her thighs and Henry's hands.

I think we held our breath for five minutes, both Edmund and I.

Inside the dimly lit room Ewa Kaludis was making love to my brother; calmly and intently, it seemed; we could only see that he was inside her for the fractions of a second when we caught sight of her whole sex, but that was enough. It was so beautiful. So bloody fucking beautiful; I imagined that in my pathetic life I'd never see anything else like it. Never again. Even though my slim, erect fourteen-year-old dick ached like a broken bone, I started to cry. As calmly and silently as when we cycled through the summer night from Lackaparken, I just let the tears flow. Standing there in the weeds and staring and crying. Crying and staring. After a while I noticed that Edmund was wanking off. He had started to breathe with his mouth open, and his right hand shot up and down like a piston in his pyjama bottoms.

I took a deep breath and started to do the same.

Afterward, we crept away. Without a word, we walked over the dewy grass down to the lake. Sauntered out on the floating dock and dived in as quietly as we could, so they wouldn't hear back at the house. Pyjama bottoms and all.

The water still as a mirror, mild and soft; I backstroked far, far out and floated for a long while. Edmund had also swum out, but he kept his distance. It was clear that we both needed space: two lonely fourteen-year-old boys in the middle of a summer night in a lake warmed by the July heat.

Edmund and I.

We hadn't exactly lost our virginities, but it was something like that. Something large and mysterious. I'd opened a door and witnessed something that I had been longing to see. Something like another country.

And it had been beautiful.

So fucking beautiful. Floating in a lake afterward was practically a requirement.

Yes, that's what I remember thinking.

12

We were on our feet first thing the next day even though we'd been awake for most of the night. Both Henry and Ewa were gone when we came down, so we assumed that he'd given her a lift in the early hours of the morning. It was understandable that she couldn't stay away for too long when she visited my brother.

Or so we assumed. More precisely, that was what we each concluded in our fourteen-year-old heads. We didn't say much that morning. Edmund stirred his cereal around the soured milk for five minutes before he took a bite. As usual. He spread whey butter on his toast with typical ceremonious fussiness. As if it were a very important task, as if it were some sort of ground-breaking scientific experiment on which depended the future of mankind. As if spreading any over the edges or leaving a square centimetre unbuttered would cause the universe to explode.

I still remember thinking that it might mean something: the difference in how we ate breakfast. Me, I usually polished off my toast and chocolate milk in under four minutes. For Edmund, breakfast was a kind of ritual, handled like the priest officiating at a communion service. Not that I had much experience of communion, but I had seen it once—when Henry was confirmed many years ago—and I'd never taken part in anything so slow or dull.

So maybe this difference in our breakfast rhythms meant something. Maybe it was one of those things that revealed our differences in character, and if one of us had been female instead of male, it would have been impossible for us to live together as man and wife. Completely out of the question.

I had to smile at that last thought. I was only speculating while I waited for Edmund to finish up that morning. Casual, daft speculation. Of course I'd never marry Edmund, however much of a woman I became; these thoughts took shape because I was tired of keeping my mind on track. That's what it was like inside my head those days. When I was alert and awake, all was well, but when I hadn't had enough sleep, anything could pop up. Cancer-Treblinka-Love ...

In any case, the weather was beautiful on this day too. We lay on the dock reading until mid-morning, and then we went out on the boat. We rowed to Fläskhällen first and played a few rounds on the new pinball machine. We didn't win a free go; it was a stingy game on the whole and slightly tilted. When we'd had enough we ate ice cream and rowed out to Seagull Shit Island. We had a rucksack filled with apple juice, a few books and *Colonel Darkin*. While Edmund ploughed through *Journey to the Centre of the Earth* for the fifth or sixth time, I tried my hand at some rather intricate panels. The image of Ewa Kaludis's swinging breasts from last night danced before my eyes, but however hard I tried, I couldn't capture it as it was in real life. I couldn't even get close. So I decided that there would be no scenes of lovemaking in *Colonel Darkin*. Now or ever. It wasn't my style, and it wasn't the Colonel's either.

When we'd taken our thirteenth dip and had opened the last apple juice Edmund put on his glasses and said: 'I have a feeling.'

It sounded serious and his expression was uncommonly earnest.

'You do?' I said.

'Yes,' said Edmund.

'What kind of feeling?'

Edmund hesitated.

'That it's all going to hell soon.'

I took a gulp of juice.

'What's going to hell?' I asked.

Edmund sighed and said that he didn't know. I waited and then asked if maybe he meant the thing between my brother and Ewa Kaludis. And Berra Albertsson.

Edmund nodded.

'I think so,' he said. 'Something is bound to happen. It can't go on like this. It's like … it's like waiting for a storm. Don't you feel it?'

I didn't answer. What my father had said that May evening at home in the kitchen on Idrottsgatan suddenly came into my mind.

A difficult summer. It's going to be a difficult summer.

Then I thought of Ewa Kaludis again. And about Mulle, unconscious. About Edmund's real father. About my mother's grey hands on top of the hospital blanket. As sombre as the colour of oatmeal streaked with blueberries.

'We'll see,' I said in the end. 'Only time will tell.'

A couple of days passed. The heat held. We swam, lay on the dock and read, rowed to Laxman's and to Fläskhällen. Everything seemed back to normal again. Henry sat in the shade and wrote and smoked his Luckys and we took care of the meals in exchange for fair compensation. Five or ten kronor. In the evenings Henry left in Killer and often didn't come home until late at night. He never said a word about Ewa Kaludis and we didn't ask either. We held our tongues and kept up a gentlemanly façade. Like Arsène Lupin. Or the Scarlet Pimpernel. Or Colonel Darkin.

'If nothing else, be a gentleman,' went one of Edmund's sayings from Ångermanland, and I agreed with him, full stop.

The next time she appeared at Gennesaret, it was 4 July. I remember the date well because Edmund and I had been talking about George Washington and the Declaration of Independence. And about President Kennedy and Jackie. It was just past ten in the evening; we'd just drunk chocolate milk and eaten a buttered rusk, as we did before bedtime; it was a bright evening and Henry was smoking constantly to keep the midges away.

I think the three of us heard the moped at the same time. Edmund and I looked at each other across the kitchen table and the clatter of the typewriter stopped. A half-minute passed until she reached the parking spot. She revved the engine and then switched it off.

'Hmm,' said Edmund. 'I think I need to take a slash.'

'Well, when you put it that way,' I said.

At first I didn't recognize her. For one flashing second, I couldn't imagine that the woman who emerged from the lilacs and ran those few steps over the grass and threw her arms around my brother was in fact Ewa Kaludis.

Ewa Kaludis/Kim Novak on the red Puch. Ewa Kaludis with the glittering eyes and the ripe, bouncing breasts. With the black slacks and the red hairband in her hair and the open Swanson shirt that fluttered in the wind.

But it was her. And she was wearing the Swanson shirt and

the slacks. Or a similar pair. But no red hairband. No glittering eyes and no wide smile. Just one eye, to be precise. The other, the right, looked as though it had been replaced by two plums. Or rather as though someone had smashed two plums where her eye was supposed to be. Her lips had changed, too. The upper lip had sort of been flattened and seemed to reach all the way up to her nose. The lower lip was large and swollen and had a wide dark line in the centre. One of her cheeks bore a large bluish stain. She looked awful and it took me a few more seconds to realize what must have happened. Someone must've done this to her. Someone had used their fists on Ewa Kaludis's face. Someone had … that someone …

I think I blacked out as soon as I pieced it together. I closed my eyes and heard Edmund hiss a curse by my side. When I looked up again Ewa Kaludis was wrapped in my brother's embrace; he held her with both arms, stroking her back, and you could see that she was crying. Henry's head was bowed down, and he was mumbling something into her hair. Her shoulders juddered as she sobbed.

Other than Edmund letting out another quivering curse, nothing happened for a while. Henry helped Ewa sit down at the table where he'd been writing, and then he turned to us.

'Listen,' he said and his eyes darted between us a few times. 'I don't care what you do, but make sure you bloody well leave us alone. Go to bed, or go row on the lake, anything, but Ewa and I have to be by ourselves now. Understood?'

I nodded. Edmund nodded.

'Good,' said Henry. 'Now, leave.'

I cast a glance at Edmund. Then we went for a piss. Then we went to bed.

She was still there the next morning.

Edmund and I had discussed the situation for the better part of the night and we both slept in. When I staggered down the stairs to get to the loo before it was too late, Ewa was sitting on one of the chairs under the ash tree wearing Henry's worn terry-towelling robe. She seemed to be freezing cold and when she hesitantly raised her hand in greeting, a lump formed in my throat that took several swallows to get rid of.

'Hi,' I said. 'I'm just going to do my morning ablutions. I'll be back in a flash.'

She did something with her face. Maybe she was trying to smile.

I peed, took a swim and returned. Edmund was still snoozing. Henry was nowhere to be seen. I took the other chair and sat down with Ewa. Across from her and to the side, quite close.

'Does it hurt?' I asked.

She shook her head carefully.

'Not so bad.'

I swallowed and tried not to look at her.

'It'll pass,' I stated. 'In a few days you'll be the most beautiful person in the world again.'

She tried to smile again. It wasn't any more successful than her previous attempt. Her lips were evidently causing her pain because she flinched and put her hand in front of her mouth.

'I look terrible,' she said. 'Please don't look at me.'

I turned my head away and studied the tree trunk instead. It was grey and rough and not particularly interesting.

'Where's Henry?' I asked.

'He went to town to buy some plasters. He'll be back soon.'

'Oh.'

We sat in silence.

'It's terrible,' I said. 'I mean, that someone would do this to you.'

She didn't answer. Just straightened up in the chair, and cleared her throat several times. I guessed that she had blood in her throat, like the victims in some of the books I'd read. It sounded like it.

'Can I get you anything?' I asked. 'Something to drink?'

She blinked a few times with her good eye.

'No, thank you,' she said. 'You're sweet, Erik.'

'Oh, it's no bother,' I said.

She cleared her throat again and wiped her forehead with the sleeve of the robe.

'You have to learn to weather the blows,' she said. 'You have to.'

'Yeah?' I said.

'Don't worry about me. I've had worse.'

'Worse?' I said.

'When I was your age,' she continued. 'And younger. I come from another country, as you may know. Just me and my sister. My parents stayed behind. We travelled across the sea in a boat, not much bigger than your rowing boat … I don't know why I'm telling you this.'

'Neither do I,' I admitted.

'Maybe it's because Henry told me about your mother,' she said after a pause. 'I know you're not having an easy time of it, Erik. I didn't know before, but I know now.'

I nodded and looked at the pattern of the bark. It hadn't changed.

'You don't like talking about it?'

I didn't answer. Ewa studied me with her good eye. Then she

leaned forward in the chair and patted the grass in front of her.

'Sit here for a moment, please.'

I hesitated at first, but then I did as she said. I floundered out of the chair and sat down on the ground between her knees. Leaned back carefully against the chair's slats. Her thighs against my sides.

'Close your eyes,' she said.

I closed my eyes. She took hold of my shoulders and gave me a gentle, slow massage.

Slow and gentle. Strong and warm. I felt dizzy inside. For all the new discoveries and experiences this summer, a hundred years must have passed since graduation at Stava School.

'Your shoulders are tense. Try to relax.'

I relaxed and became like putty in her hands. I got an erection of course, but I made sure that it couldn't really be seen through my baggy swimming trunks. Then I gave into the pleasure of sitting between Ewa's legs, enjoying her hands. I realized that I'd started to cry again, but that this time there weren't any tears. Just a lovely, gentle buzz behind my eyes, and for a clear, flashing second I knew what it was like to be Henry.

My brother Henry.

Eventually Edmund woke, and eventually Henry returned from his trip to the pharmacy, but that didn't matter. When Ewa let go of my shoulders and mussed my hair it felt as if we'd entered into a sworn brotherhood. Or had made some sort of secret pact. We hadn't spoken much—not at all, really. We were just sitting in the grass together, but still it was something else, as Edmund might have said.

Something bloody else. I thought about it once or twice a day in the time leading up to the Incident, and every time I did, a strong, warm feeling filled me. Warm and strong just like her hands on my tense shoulders.

The feeling of slipping into a nice warm bath after a cold winter's day, I know that's what I thought then.

But it sort of radiated from within.

13

Henry left with Ewa that night. I think he rode the Puch while Ewa drove Killer; it must be harder to drive a moped than to drive a car when you only have one working eye. In any case, the parking area was empty when Edmund and I returned from a long bike ride around ten.

Then another couple of days passed. The weather volleyed between sun and rain. But it was generally quite warm. We tried to go fishing, but Möckeln had a reputation for being dead when it came to fish, and neither Edmund nor I were particularly amused by sitting around and staring at a float.

Even less amused, in fact, by the thought of having to reel in a poor dace or perch and stick a knife in it. Or whack it until it died. Or whatever you did to fish.

As luck would have it we never needed to come up with a solution to the problem because we didn't get one to bite.

But Edmund did get strep throat. A mild case—according to his own diagnosis; he'd had strep throat a few times before—but he still was lethargic and feverish and preferred to sleep. Or read.

'Read, sleep, drink,' he said. 'From these threads, my wellness is woven.'

'An idiom from the heart of Lapland?' I asked.

'Not exactly,' said Edmund. 'My dad says that.'

124

'Your real one?'

'No, for Christ's sake,' said Edmund. 'Not him. Only crap comes from him.'

Those days it was harder than usual to talk to Henry. When he wasn't running errands in Killer, he mostly went around muttering and smoking. His writing didn't seem to be moving forward either; he often just sat staring at the Facit, as if he were trying convince it to write the existential novel itself. Sometimes I heard him curse and tear a sheet of paper out of the roller. He was constantly grumbling and irate.

Because both my brother and Edmund were busy—Edmund with his strep throat, Henry with other things—I also kept to myself. I drew more than ten pages of *Colonel Darkin and the Mysterious Heiress* and was chuffed with the result. Since I had decided to censor all the half-naked female bodies, it was much easier to get on with the story. I guess that's how it is, I thought, glumly. As in literature, so in life.

During those days, the meals were monotonous, too. Edmund had lost his appetite and when Henry ate, he didn't care what he put in his mouth. You could just as well have set a plate of moss on the table for him. Because of this and the situation in general, we mostly ate potatoes with butter. We placed two jars of herring on the table at every meal, but none of us bothered to twist off the lid of either of them and take a whiff.

It was what it was, and we had plenty of potatoes in stock.

I'd just finished *And Then There Were None* and had turned to the wall to sleep, when I heard them walking across the lawn.

Henry and Ewa. I looked at my self-illuminating watch. Twelve thirty. Edmund was breathing heavily with his mouth open over in his bed. It was a blustery day and every now and then a tree branch swished against the window. I couldn't help but think how safe and secure it felt lying in a warm bed. How free from danger.

Well, only for as long as you were lying in bed. The reality beyond the bed was another matter. Something else. The simple act of putting your feet on the cold floor and then going out into the world meant that you were exposing yourself to a plethora of risks and dangers. There were Henrys and Ewas and Edmunds. But also black eyes and swollen lips and fists that were as hard and merciless as stone. Decisions that had to be made and matters that had to be handled whether you wanted to or not. Dads who hit and Treblinkas and cancerous tumours that grew and grew.

Out in the world. Beyond the bed, on the floor. I rolled over and pulled the blanket around me more tightly. I could hear Henry and Ewa speaking softly down below. No music tonight, apparently. No rhythmic creaking of the bed or libertine whimpering. I knew this wasn't that kind of night. This night was different.

I wondered what they were talking about. I thought about that trick detectives used in the movies where they place a glass against the wall so they can listen in on conversations in the adjoining room. If that really did work, it could work against the floor as well.

There was a half-full glass next to Edmund's bed. Drinking plenty of liquids was part of his war against strep throat, so if I wanted to test it out, I could; if I really wanted to know what Ewa and Henry were talking about down there, I wouldn't have to make too much of an effort. Open the window and toss out the apple juice. And then lie on the floor with the glass against the wooden boards and my ear against it. Easy as pie.

I couldn't be bothered. Maybe I was too tired. Maybe I felt it wouldn't be gentlemanly.

If nothing else, be a gentleman.

It wasn't a bad rule to live by, we'd decided, Edmund and I. The gentility of standing in the flower bed and wanking to Ewa and Henry the other night was debatable, but surely even a gentleman was allowed a day off. Like the sun has its spots.

I was musing from the comfort of my own bed. The voices down below only reached me as a distant mumbling and when I finally drifted off, my dream silenced Henry's grave voice. I only heard Ewa's and she was speaking to me. She sat next to me in bed, or rather, behind me and to the side, and she was massaging my tense shoulders.

My shoulders and other things. I wouldn't have minded if I'd never woken from that dream.

The next morning, there was a note on the kitchen table that read 'Have a lot to take care of. Will be back before midnight. Meatballs and peaches in the larder. Henry.'

It wasn't like my brother to leave a note about what he was up to, and I guessed Ewa Kaludis was behind it. Henry wasn't usually away from Gennesaret for more than six or eight hours at a time and now he would be gone both day and night, apparently, but it still wasn't like him leave a note like this. Not my brother.

I checked to see if there really were two tins on the shelf in the larder. There were. One with Mother Elna's moose meatballs in a creamy sauce. One with halved pears in thick syrup. It didn't sound bad, even if I didn't really see the point of the syrup. If Edmund's lack of appetite held strong, I could—if nothing else—look forward to a decent tuck-in later in the day. Shame there wasn't any cream for the peaches, but cycling or rowing all the way to Laxman's for a splash of cream seemed excessive. Not worth worrying about with the clouds of unease that had been rolling in lately.

It was quite a listless day. To begin with, at least. Edmund was on the mend, he said, but only slightly. It would probably take another day or two to be rid of the sodding strep, he figured.

Sleep, read and drink, then. Absolutely no outings. Not to Laxman's, not anywhere. There were no two ways about it, he had no desire to get out of bed. He was 'convalescing', as they liked to say in Västerbotten.

I placed two bottles of apple juice on the table, and wished him well and went outside and sat on one of the loungers with *Darkin* and a new Agatha Christie. The last one hadn't been bad; the new one was called *The Murder of Roger Ackroyd* and Edmund said it was a super story.

And that was essentially how I spent the day before the Incident.

Sitting in the sun lounger with *Colonel Darkin* and Agatha Christie. Edmund came out a few times, but when it was sunny he thought it was too hot and when clouds covered the sun he froze. He complained that he was having a hard time with books as well, because he kept forgetting the pages he read before he fell asleep and had to start again when he woke. I suggested he try *Journey to the Centre of the Earth* once more—you could make sense of that one backward and upside-down—but he said he wasn't in the mood for Jules Verne. He needed something like Patrick Quentin and Ellery Queen, and you could definitely read crime novels more than once.

Except certain ones, of course.

I prepared the moose meatballs in the middle of the afternoon. I ate nine; Edmund ate one. We split the peaches between us more evenly, four–two. All in all, I was satisfied with my meal.

Even though I had to prepare it *and* do the washing up.

Just as I had finished with the latter, we received our first caller of the afternoon. Gladys Lundin walked across the property clearing her throat and coughing, asking if we had any schnapps to spare.

Normal people, like Benny's mum and Mrs. Lundmark two floors up on Idrottsgatan, would sometimes knock and ask for a cup of sugar or flour for pancakes or rhubarb pie, but the Lundins were not normal people. Far from it. As far as I knew, Gladys was the matriarch of the tribe; she was at least seventy and probably weighed more than a bit over a hundred kilos. She propelled herself forward with two sturdy oak canes and always had a lit cigarette dangling from the corner of her mouth. None of this prevented her from coming over and begging for schnapps when the need struck.

I explained that we didn't have any alcohol in the house at the moment, and so she asked for a kilo of potatoes instead.

I could hardly deny her that, because we had half a crate. With the canes and the cigarettes, the carrying became complicated, but in the end I hung a bowl on a cord around her neck. She hobbled away without saying thank you and I wondered if she was going to sit down and make schnapps with the potatoes as soon as she got home. I only had a vague idea of the process, but with some luck she might distil a glass by the evening.

From that day forward, I thought it was strange that they

showed up so soon after each other, Gladys Lundin and the next visitor, but whichever way I looked at it, I couldn't find a logical connection.

But never mind; after getting rid of Gladys I hadn't been in the chair for more than twenty minutes before I heard another cough behind me. Much stronger and much more ominous.

I rose to my feet and then I was eyeball-to-eyeball with Bertil Albertsson. Super-Berra. The man who had such a strong arm that if a ball he threw hit a goalkeeper, the impact would be fatal. The man who had hung his striped blazer nonchalantly on one finger and handed it to Atle Eriksson before he started the battle royal against red-faced Mulle in Lackaparken.

The man whose fiancée was called Ewa Kaludis.

I dropped *Colonel Darkin* in the grass but I didn't think to pick it up. Tried to swallow; it wasn't easy and I wondered if Edmund had given me his strep throat. Berra stood before me with the same wide stance that he'd employed at Lackaparken. He wore a white, short-sleeved shirt and his tanned, hairy arms rippled with muscles and veins. His rough-hewn face was inscrutable; he had one eyebrow raised a few centimetres, and he looked at me as if I was something he happened to have stepped on in the gutter.

'Hi,' I said.

He didn't reply. His eyebrow stayed just below his hairline, but his jaw was moving slightly. Grinding. I couldn't think of anything to say, so I tried to stare back. No use.

'Where's your brother?' he said in the end. Without moving his lips.

'Who?' I asked.

I don't know how I came up with such a daft question, but I think I was trying to buy some time. Time to faint, or time

130

for some merciful god or goddess to come to my rescue. To arrive at Gennesaret and carry me away to a desert island in the South Seas for all eternity.

No god appeared and I didn't faint.

'Your brother,' Berra Albertsson repeated. 'Henry. I have a few things to say to him.'

'Oh, him,' I said.

'How many brothers do you have?' asked Berra.

'Just one,' I said.

'And where is he, then?'

'He's not in,' I said.

'When will he be back?'

'I don't know. Late.'

'Late?'

'Tonight. Twelve. Or even later. He left a note.'

'Tonight.'

'Yes.'

'Hmm.' He lowered his eyebrow. Coughed twice and spat on the lawn. The gob landed twenty centimetres from my left foot. Five centimetres from *Colonel Darkin*.

'Tell him,' he said. 'Tell him that I'll be back at one tonight. There are some things I want to discuss with him.'

'He might not be here then either,' I said. 'He might be even later.'

'Then I'll wait.'

And with that he left. I stayed still and watched him. When he'd disappeared behind the lilac bushes, I lowered my gaze and looked at the gob of spit that lay glittering in the grass.

It's never going to go away, I thought. That damned gob is going to be on Gennesaret's lawn one hundred years from now. It is what it is.

'Who were you talking to?' Edmund stuck his head out of the window. 'I was sleeping and then I heard voices. Who was here?'

Edmund went as pale as a corpse when I told him about my conversation with Berra Albertsson.

He took off his glasses and put them back on again ten times and he gnashed his teeth, but mostly he looked frightened. Dogged and focused in spite of the fever, but also confused. This must have been what it was like when he was waiting for his real dad to come and whack him with the belt. He barely said a word while I recounted what Berra had said and what I'd said. Clasped and unclasped his hands and then tried to swallow, but that was all. He had no idea what we should do.

Not one.

'The storm,' he finally said. 'I told you. We've been waiting for the storm and now it's here.'

'Goddammit,' I said, because I didn't know what to say and I felt that I needed to buck myself up with a few swear words. 'Damn it all to hell.'

'Exactly,' said Edmund.

The rain started to fall around eight p.m. and I kept Edmund company by going to bed a little after nine. It was a proper storm. Bright streaks of lightning and thunder claps too close for comfort. It seemed like it would never end.

'Some storms go round and round,' Edmund commented. 'In Ånger once the thunder and lightning went on for over twelve bloody hours non-stop. It can make you feel quite small, actually.'

'How's the strep?' I asked, because I didn't want to talk about the storm. It was bad enough as it was.

'A bit better, I'm sure,' Edmund stated after a few test swallows. 'I'll probably have recovered by tomorrow.'

But ten minutes later he was sleeping like a log. I turned off the light and lay awake listening to the rain on the roof and the rumbling. The lightning kept striking fifteen or thirty seconds before the rumbling began, so perhaps it was as Edmund had said.

The storm was hanging around and circling us.

And it did make you feel rather small.

Then I must have fallen asleep, because soon after twelve I woke. The rain had stopped but there was a lively wind.

I heard Henry turn on the tape deck downstairs and I think he was talking to someone.

Edmund's bed was empty.

II

14

It was Lasse Crook-mouth who found the body, and it was Lasse Crook-mouth who landed on the front page of *Kurren* two days in a row. His parents had a cottage in Sjölycke where Crook-mouth also spent most of the summer. It was a well-known fact that he dreamed of becoming a competitive cyclist. Like Harry Snell. Or Ove Adamsson. His face ruled out any chance of him becoming a film star or a trumpet player, but nothing was keeping him from being a speed-demon on wheels.

He had been in the town's junior league for a few seasons and was expected to move up to the seniors in a year or so. A rising star, as they say in sports. Crook-mouth had all the prerequisites—everyone who knew anything about cycling agreed—and his face was not an obstacle.

Given his ambition, Crook-mouth took advantage of the summer days for training, and in the wee hours of the morning he would take his racing bike out of the shed in Sjölycke and hit the road for a fifty- to sixty-kilometre ride. Or eighty or a hundred if he was on top form—and this was one of those days. Riding the uneven gravel roads wasn't a usual part of his routine because there was a clear risk of skidding and flat tyres.

But that morning he did. Just for variety's sake, I suppose, there was still the odd race track on gravel at this time. In the dawning sixties.

He took the road that led east through the woods, toward the Levis, and it turned out to be an especially short spin.

Short and so goddamn shocking, as he later told the journalist from *Kurren*. Only a few kilometres into the ride, he comes charging down the winding road past ours and the Lundins' parking spots. Full speed. Bent over the handlebars. Sees two parked vehicles. A black VW and a red Volvo PV 1800.

The Volvo makes him brake so sharply that he's practically standing on his ears in the gravel on the road.

Or rather, what's next to the car does.

The passenger's door is open and just below it on the ground a person is lying on their stomach. It's a man wearing narrow black shoes, light polyester trousers and a white short-sleeved shirt. This is what Crook-mouth sees when he turns his bike around and goes back up the hill. He glimpses a striped blazer on the driver's seat. The man is lying on his front, but slightly contorted, with his arms stretched alongside his body. As Crook-mouth says to the reporters and the photographers several times: The arms were what made it click.

Something wasn't right.

A living person doesn't lie like that. You can tell at a glance, at least if you have a pair of eyes in your head, and Crook-mouth certainly does. It's around quarter past six and he's guiding his racing bike toward the unbelievable thing with great caution and care.

Sees what he already knows.

Sees that the man lying there has a gaping hole in his head, and that it's covered in blood: his hair, his shirt and the ground around him.

He can't tell who it is, because of course he doesn't dare touch the body and turn it over. You're not supposed to do that, anyway. It's the police's job to turn dead bodies over, not Lasse Crook-mouth's.

No, Crook-mouth doesn't identify the man in the clearing; we do. Henry and Edmund and I, because we're the ones he comes running to, shouting at the top of his lungs.

And it's we who run with him up the path, and we who stand in a semi-circle around Bertil 'Berra' Albertsson, and not one of us says a word.

Not one of us. Three of us know that it's Super-Berra who's lying there, but none of us lets anything slip. Not one sound.

Neither does Lasse Crook-mouth. For thirty seconds, four people stand there, staring at a fifth who is no longer a person, and these are the longest thirty seconds of our lives.

Then we look at the clock and see that it's six twenty-five. It's the morning of 12 July and the Incident is a fact.

When Lasse Crook-mouth left to go and call the police from the Lundins', I knew there was something I had to find out, even though my head felt scrambled. I managed to make eye contact with my brother Henry and to mouth the question 'Ewa?', looking in the direction of Gennesaret. I don't know why I felt I had to keep Edmund out of it, but I did. It was as if this had to stay between me and my brother. This, whatever it was.

I think Henry understood me, but he didn't answer. He simply shook his head gently and lit a Lucky Strike.

I sighed and put my arm around Edmund. He was shivering in the cold morning air, but otherwise, it was just as he'd predicted.

The strep throat had eased during the night.

15

The first police car arrived while we were still by the parking
spot. Crook-mouth had returned—along with Gladys Lundin
and a woman about thirty years her junior who was her double. Smaller and paler, she didn't have a cane yet, but she was
valiantly chain-smoking and her breasts were already droop-
ing down toward her belly button.

'That's the way that cookie crumbled,' was Gladys's first comment. 'Lucky none of the men are home, or the cops would
pop straight down and pick them up.'

No one else had an opinion about the situation. Super-Berra
lay where he lay on the gravel, but no one seemed to want to
take a closer look. We spread out in a protective semi-circle
of sorts, with our backs to the Incident, and when the black
and white Amazon turned up with three uniformed police-
men and one in plain clothes inside, we had to give them our
names and then trudge home and sit tight.

'Goddamn,' said Edmund when we were back in our room.
'Goddamn.'

I realized that I was feeling very sick and considered going
into the woods and sticking a finger down my throat, but the
waves of nausea retreated. I shut my eyes and hoped that I
could sleep for an hour or two, but that was wishful thinking.
From the ground floor, I heard Henry sit down at the Facit

and begin to write; I thought it was strange that he'd do that at a time like this, and indeed the clatter stopped after a few minutes.

'Hey, Erik,' said Edmund.

'Yes?' I said.

'Let's not talk about it now. I can't hack it.'

'All right,' I said. 'It'd probably be a good thing if we got some rest first.'

'He's dead,' Edmund said anyway. 'Can you believe the bastard is dead?'

'Yes,' I said. 'Berra Albertsson is dead.'

The detective arrived around nine. He was called Lindström and wore a pale suit and a bow tie, and, except for his black, slicked-back hair, resembled Ture Sventon, P.I.

One at a time, he greeted us: shook hands and then said his name, Detective Superintendent Verner Lindström, three times. He smelled faintly of cologne and spoke carefully and thoughtfully, as if he were making an effort to discard any unnecessary and frivolous words before speaking so he could be sure to say exactly what he meant. He exuded a certain confidence, and I saw that he wasn't to be toyed with.

Naturally, he started with Henry. They locked themselves away in the kitchen and while Edmund and I wandered around the house, we could see them sitting in there at the table covered with the checked wax cloth, like two chess players.

Because we didn't really know what to do with ourselves, we went up to the clearing to have a look.

Four other cars had arrived at the scene; it had been cordoned off and on black and yellow signs it read that a crime scene investigation was under way and it was forbidden for unauthorized persons to cross the police line. Edmund explained to a cocky constable that we were the ones who had found the body—almost, if you didn't count Lasse Crook-mouth—but that didn't help. We had no business being there. Still, I noticed that Berra Albertsson's body had been removed and thick chalk lines had been drawn around where it had lain.

I also saw several men in green overalls crawling in and around the red Volvo. They wore thin gloves and held brushes and magnifying glasses. Suddenly, the scene felt so unreal that I had to pinch myself in the arm to make sure I wasn't dreaming. Edmund noticed what I was doing and shook his head grimly.

'It won't help,' he stated. 'You might as well accept you're awake, mate.'

A number of others were milling about outside the barrier, but not many. I saw Crook-mouth and his dad, the old Levi couple and a few folk from Sjölycke. As well as a couple of journalists and a photographer.

But not many, as I said. I guessed that the world didn't yet know that the handball legend Berra Albertsson was dead. You could still tell yourself that nothing had happened. Almost.

But that feeling wouldn't last long; and then I realized that Henry's Killer was inside the police ropes and placards and for some reason I felt so cold that I started to shiver.

Yes, I must've been awake this whole time.

When we arrived back at Gennesaret, Henry's interrogation was finished. It was Edmund's and my turn to sit at the kitchen table with Detective Lindström. Before we went inside I began to think about when Berra and I had talked out on the lawn not twenty-four hours ago.

'I'm just going to check on something,' I said to Edmund and left him for a few seconds.

It was as I thought. There wasn't a trace of the gob.

'As you know, there has been a serious incident,' the detective began. 'It's important that everyone's statement is as accurate as possible so that we can sort this out. No guesses. No lies. Is that clear?'

Edmund and I nodded.

'Your names, please.'

We gave them.

'And you're living here this summer?'

'Yes,' I said.

'Together with Henry Wassman, who is also your brother?'

'Yes.'

'What time did you go to bed last night?'

Edmund explained that he had gone to bed at half eight because of his strep throat. I said I was in bed about half an hour later.

Detective Lindström didn't have a tape recorder, but he wrote down every word we said with a blue biro in a notepad that lay in front of him on the table. He kept one arm bent protectively around the pad, so it was impossible to read his writing. You could tell it wasn't his first time questioning someone, and my respect for him grew.

'And what time did you fall asleep, approximately?'

'At once,' explained Edmund.

I hesitated.

'Ten, I think.'

'Was either of you awake later during the night?'

Edmund wrinkled his forehead for a moment and I let him answer first.

'I went out for a pee,' he said.

'At what time?'

'No idea,' said Edmund. 'Haven't the foggiest.'

'And you didn't notice anything unusual then?'

'No,' said Edmund. 'Nothing.'

'Was it raining?'

Edmund thought about it.

'No,' he said. 'It wasn't raining.'

Detective Lindström made a note.

'And you?' he said, turning to me. 'Were you awake at any point during the night?'

'No,' I said. 'I don't think so.'

'Not at all?'

'No.'

'Was your brother at home last night?'

'No.'

'What time did he come home?'

'I don't know. Not while I was awake, in any case.'

He turned to Edmund again.

'Did you notice if Henry was home when you were relieving yourself?'

'No idea,' said Edmund.

'You didn't see if his light was on?'

'I think it was off. Why don't you ask Henry when he came home yourself, Detective Lindström, sir?'

Lindström didn't bother to answer. Instead, he set his sights on me.

'And there's nothing else that you think we should know about?'

'No.'

He wrote a few words on the pad.

'Tell me what happened this morning,' he then said.

Edmund and I took turns retelling how Lasse Crook-mouth's shouts from down on the lawn had woken us. How, together with him and Henry, we'd rushed up to the parking area to see what had happened. How we'd waited there while Crook-mouth called the police from the Lundins'.

'Do you know who was on the ground?' asked Lindström.

Edmund and I looked at each other.

'Yes,' I said. 'It was Berra Albertsson.'

Lindström nodded.

'Did you know this already then? When you saw him.'

'Yes.'

'How come you recognized him?'

'We had seen him before,' said Edmund.

'Where?' said Lindström.

'Around,' said Edmund. 'In Lackaparken, for example.'

'He's been in the papers, too,' I added. 'In *Kurren*.'

Lindström adjusted his bow tie and made a note. Leaned back and thought for a few seconds.

'He hadn't paid you a visit?'

'Berra Albertsson?' said Edmund. 'No, he hasn't.'

'Never,' I said. 'Not when I've been home, at least.'

'Do you know if your brother was acquainted with him?'

'No,' I said. 'I'm sure he wasn't.'

'Have you seen him around? In Sjölycke or anywhere around Möckeln?'

We thought about it.

'No,' said Edmund.

'No,' I said.

Lindström took a tube of Bronzol out of his inner pocket and shook out two pastilles. Weighed them for a few seconds in his hand and then threw them in his mouth with a practised gesture.

'Are you sure? Are you sure you've never seen Berra Albertsson in the area?'

'Absolutely,' said Edmund.

'Only in Lackaparken,' I said.

'And you didn't hear anything unusual last night?'

We shook our heads. Detective Lindström chewed on the Bronzol pastilles, deep in thought.

'All right then,' he said and then the interrogation was over.

Our fathers took the twelve o'clock bus and Laxman picked them up in his yellow taxi from Åsbro.

'You can't stay here,' said my father.

'It's out of the question,' said Edmund's.

'Take it easy,' said Henry.

Edmund's dad took out a handkerchief that was as big as a tent and patted his face and neck.

'Easy?' he snorted. 'How the heck can we take it easy? A murder was committed one hundred metres from here. Are you mad?'

He looked at Henry with wide-open eyes, and when Henry didn't answer he turned to my father.

'Is he mad?'

'You have to go back to town,' my father repeated. 'This won't work. It's unbelievable. Nothing like this has ever happened before.'

Henry lit a Lucky Strike and got up from the kitchen table.

'Do what you like with the lads,' he retorted. 'I'm staying here.'

'You want to go home, right, boys?' asked Edmund's dad in a milder tone. 'You do want to get back to town as soon as possible?'

I looked at Edmund. Edmund looked at me.

'Not on your life,' said Edmund.

'Unbelievable,' my father repeated. 'I'm speechless.'

'Don't you understand? A murderer is on the loose!' said Mr. Wester.

They stayed the whole day and spent the night, and the next day Edmund and I agreed to go back to town with them if they promised that we could return to Gennesaret the day after, as long as no other act of violence was committed around Möckeln. Edmund went home, and I went with my father to the hospital and sat for an hour with my mother. Her hair had been washed and set, but otherwise she seemed unchanged. Perhaps she was paler. We spoke about Berra Albertsson's murder the entire time—the newspapers had dedicated several pages to it—or, more precisely, my mother and father talked about it while I mostly sat in silence, nodding and pretending to agree with everything they said. The results from the doctors' latest tests weren't ready yet, so there wasn't really much else to discuss. It was what it was.

Before we left the hospital my mother took my hand and held it between both of hers for a while. She looked at me with a kind of gravity and I thought she might share another one of her strange words of wisdom.

She didn't.

'Take care of yourself, my boy,' is all she said. 'Take care of yourself and take care of Edmund, too.'

We went home on the eight o'clock bus. Then I slept one

night at Idrottsgatan and the next day, a Saturday, Henry came and picked Edmund and me up and we returned to Gennesaret.

16

Even though we were so close to the heart of the action, we had to read *Kurren* and the *Läns* newspaper to find out about the police's progress with the case. On the first day, Police Chief Elmestrand explained that there was a good chance of finding the perpetrator in the near future, and they had no intention of calling in the National Criminal Investigation Department. He had total faith in Detective Lindström and his men, he said, but the ever-vigilant general public was welcome to share any information that might shed more light in the case. It was important that everyone did their part to help solve this brutal tragedy that had befallen our region and the Swedish sporting community.

The national handball team had been dealt a blow, as Bejman put it in the *Läns* newspaper.

With regard to the suspect's identity, the police didn't have any answers on that Saturday. They said they were pursuing several leads, but it was too soon to focus their suspicions on any one person.

Perhaps it was the work of a madman. Perhaps there were other motives.

According to the facts that were reported in the papers, it was assumed that Bertil 'Berra' Albertsson had met his killer some time between twelve and two on the night between

Wednesday and Thursday. Apparently, the perpetrator had launched his attack just as Albertsson was getting out of his vehicle in the small parking area where he was later found—next to the gravel road that ran through the forest between the Sjölycke resort and the Fläskhällen beach on Lake Möckeln. They were still in the dark about what Albertsson had been doing there at that time of day. In spite of the information provided by people who had known the deceased—his fiancée Ewa Kaludis, for instance—nothing had surfaced that could shed light on the matter.

The murder itself had been committed with a so-called blunt object, probably a heavy hammer or a small sledgehammer. A single blow had been enough; it had made contact with Albertsson's head from above, cracking through the crown of his skull to the brain. It was assumed that he died instantly.

'Right in the nut,' said Edmund as he set *Kurren* aside. 'Shall we go for a swim?'

From the start, Edmund and I seemed to have an understanding. An unspoken understanding that we wouldn't talk about the murder. At least not more than absolutely necessary. But neither of us could stop thinking about it; it overshadowed everything else. The Incident occupied every nook and cranny of our minds, all of the time.

It was far too much to process. That was clear without even having to talk about it.

Edmund and I had a lot of unspoken understandings. It felt both completely natural and a bit strange. Although we hadn't spent more than a couple months together, we knew where we stood with each other. It was as if we had known each other our entire lives. We could have been twins, I thought once.

But Ewa Kaludis was a different matter. We had to put her on the agenda now and then.

'I wonder,' said Edmund. 'I wonder what she said to the police about her black eye?'

'She's probably not feeling particularly well at the moment,' I said.

'Must be lonely,' said Edmund. 'Without Henry and all that. You don't think they're seeing each other?'

'I should think not,' I said.

The idea of looking her up had already started to sprout in the back of my mind. In Edmund's, too, apparently.

On Sunday Detective Lindström returned. He didn't stay more than an hour, but he spoke with all three of us. One after the other, and this time to me and Edmund separately.

'This is about a couple of details,' he explained when it was my turn.

'Details?' I said.

'Details,' said Lindström. 'They might seem insignificant, but the whole picture always comes together through the details.'

'Only time will tell,' I said.

He furrowed his brow for a moment. Then he turned a page in his notebook and clicked his biro several times.

'Do you have many tools out here?'

'Tools?'

'Saws, axes, hammers and the like.'

'Well,' I said. 'Some, not many.'

'We are mainly interested in a large hammer or a small sledgehammer.'

'I see.'

'Do you know if you have one like that?'

I thought back.

'There's a hammer in the tool box,' I said. 'But it's not big.'

'Is it this one?'

He lifted up a hammer that he'd been hiding under the table. I glanced at it.

'Yes.'

'Are you certain?'

I looked at it more closely.

'Yes, that's the one. We used it when we built the dock; I recognize it.'

'Good,' said Lindström. 'That's what your friend said, too.'

I didn't answer.

'There isn't a larger one?'

'Yes, there is,' I said. 'I think there's a small sledgehammer or something out in the shed.'

'Is there?' said Lindström. 'Shall we go take a look?'

I followed him out to the tumbledown shed next to the privy. Unlatched the door and looked in at the mess.

'I don't know where it is.'

I poked around inside.

'Can't you find it?' Lindström wondered. He had taken out his tube of Bronzol and was rocking from heel to toe.

'Don't think so.'

'It doesn't matter. I don't believe it's here. Your brother couldn't find it either. You don't happen to know where it might have gone?'

I climbed out of the shed and brushed off the dust.

'No,' I said. 'I don't.'

'Do you remember when you saw it last?'

I shrugged.

'Dunno. A few weeks ago, maybe.'

'You didn't use it when you were building the dock?'

'No.'

We went back to the kitchen table.

'The other detail,' Lindström said after writing in his notepad. 'The other detail concerns a certain Miss Ewa Kaludis.'

'Oh?'

'Are you acquainted with her?'

'She was a supply teacher at school,' I said. 'In May and June. But only for a few subjects. Our usual teacher had broken her leg.'

Lindström nodded.

'Was she a good teacher?'

'Well, yes. I suppose she was.'

'Did you know that she kept company with Berra Albertsson?'

'Yes.'

'Have you seen her at all this summer?'

'No,' I said. 'Oh, yes actually. Once in Lackaparken.'

'Lackaparken?'

'Yes.'

'Only there?'

'Yes.'

'Not on any other occasion?'

'No.'

'Are you sure?'

I thought about it.

'Not that I remember,' I said.

Lindström was silent for a few seconds and didn't make any notes. Then he stood up.

'I think I'll need to stop by again,' he said. 'If you find that sledgehammer, I want you to get in touch.'

'I will,' I promised.

We shook hands and he was on his way.

Once in fourth grade Balthazar Lindblom wet himself. It happened during RE class with a supply teacher called Rockgård, whom we called Rockhard, because he was. He was incorruptible. It was no use trying to be cheeky or doing things differently from how he'd decided.

Balthazar had his accident around ten minutes before the lesson finished, and because we were silently working from our books, everyone noticed the gushing sound coming from under his desk.

Even Rockhard.

'I beg your pardon,' he barked. 'What are you doing, you imbecile?'

Balthazar finished peeing before answering. The puddle spread out into a small lake, and those of us who were sitting near him had to lift our feet.

'Teacher said so,' said Balthazar.

'What?' said Rockhard. 'What do you mean?'

'Teacher said that we had to make sure to visit the toilet during break. That there was no point in asking to go during the lesson.'

It was probably the only time in his teaching career that Rockhard ended his class ten minutes before the bell.

And Balthazar Lindblom is the only person I know that managed to become some sort of hero—if only for a short time—just by pissing himself.

With time it wasn't so much the act of peeing, but Rockhard's comment that stuck in my mind. What he said before he ushered us out into the playground, that is.

'Perfect. You handled this perfectly, my boy.'

I thought of Rockhard when Detective Superintendent Lindström left Gennesaret that Sunday afternoon. Not because they were especially similar, either in their manner or in their looks, but they still had something in common. Something incorruptible. Something that was useless to try to change or oppose.

I didn't know if this was for better or worse.

To be honest, it was the first time that summer that Britt Laxman paid us any attention. Edmund and me. That Monday morning, I mean, when we walked under the ringing bell into the shop in Åsbro.

The first and only time, actually.

'Well, hello there,' she said. Flashing her teeth and losing interest in the grey-haired woman at the counter airing her complaints. 'Hi Erik, hi Edmund. How's it going?'

At least she had learned our names. I looked at Edmund and around the shop. It was unusually crowded. I could tell that Britt Laxman wasn't the only one who knew who we were. I could tell that most of them weren't there to do their shopping. The sudden silence and tongue-tiedness were connected to our arrival, that was as clear as day. While it was flattering, it was also threatening, and I think Edmund felt the same.

Three seconds, it wasn't longer than that, but it was enough. We looked at each other knowingly. Old Major Casselmiolke cleared his throat and continued the train of thought that he'd begun with Moppe Nilsson at the meat counter.

'Tracks!' thundered the military man. 'There have to be tracks! Clues, for heaven's sake! They're just waiting for the analysis! We live in a scientific age, don't you forget that!'

'I'm afraid I don't agree,' Moppe countered leisurely while moving the sausages around with his sausage-like fingers. 'I think the perpetrator should thank God for the rain.'

'The rain?' said Casselmiolke. 'God?'

As if he'd never heard of those things.

'The rain that fell between four and five in the morning,' Moppe explained. 'It would have washed away every last clue. That's what it said in *Aftonbladet* this Saturday.'

'*Aftonbladet*?' said Casselmiolke. 'Dreadful rag! You don't happen to have a copy, do you?'

'I'm sorry, no,' Britt Laxman called from across the store. 'They sold out in half an hour.' Then she turned to us wide-eyed and with a fresh smile. 'What'll it be?' she asked. 'How are you both doing?'

We went through the shopping list as quickly as we could, but when we were done, she didn't want to let us go.

'What do you think?' she lowered her voice—to avoid every last person in the shop hearing her. 'Who did it?'

Edmund cast a glance at me.

'A madman,' he then said. 'Some nutjob who escaped from a loony bin. Isn't that obvious?'

And that was the line we continued to toe. The madman-line. When people asked us what we thought—and that happened every so often, God knows: we'd seen the body, we lived right by the scene of the crime after all, we must've heard something in the night, and so on—yes, then we went with the lunatic theory. A madman. An escaped mental patient. Only someone who was out of his mind could've been behind the murder of Bertil 'Berra' Albertsson. Of course. Anything else was unthinkable.

We knew instantly—as soon as we were back on Laxman's steps, and without having to discuss it—that this had been exactly the right response.

A madman.

Who else?

17

Those nights, I was dreaming about Ewa Kaludis again. Sometimes she had a black eye, sometimes not. I sensed that Edmund was also lying in bed dreaming of her, and when I asked him, he wasn't shy about admitting it.

'Of course,' he said. 'She's got her hooks in me. Britt Laxman feels sort of stale now.'

'Britt Laxman?' I said. 'You're not saying you used to dream about her?'

'Well,' said Edmund. 'Not dream, exactly. Fantasize.'

Soon we were talking about if it was possible for two people to dream the same dream. Could Edmund and I lie, each in our own bed, and be looking at the same images of Ewa Kaludis? As if we were sitting in the cinema watching the same film?

It seemed to make sense. The dream factory might have some sort of rationing programme and there simply weren't enough unique dreams to go around for each person every night.

But Edmund disagreed.

'They can't be that bloody stingy in the dream world,' he said. 'It's only in our crap world that you have to go around niggling and skimping. Can't we at least have our dreams to ourselves?'

A dream for each person?

I hoped that Edmund was right. It sounded fair and democratic—as Brylle would say during social studies. As for our nightmares, we never discussed them.

After the murder my brother Henry stuck closer to Gennesaret than before, but he was hardly more talkative. He didn't write much either; mostly he lay on his bed, reading what he'd already written, I think. He took Killer out for short spins and went for a row on the lake a few times, too. But he was rarely gone for more than an hour. On Tuesday morning, he explained that he had to go to Örebro and that he'd be away for a while. He set off soon after twelve, and Edmund and I decided that we'd give the pinball machine down at Fläskhällen another go. We were just about to push off in the boat when a man appeared around the side of the house.

He appeared to be in his thirties. But with thinning hair. He wore a white nylon shirt and sunglasses and was signalling for us to come back by waving both of his arms.

We looked at each other and went ashore again.

'Lundberg,' he said when we came up to him. 'Rogga Lundberg. I'm looking for Henry Wassman.'

I introduced myself and explained that Henry wasn't at home. And that he'd probably be away a while.

'Aha,' said Rogga Lundberg. 'You're his little brother, aren't you?'

I didn't like him. From the very first moment, I knew that Rogga Lundberg was no good and that we had to get rid of him as quickly as possible. Maybe it was the sunglasses that gave away his unsavoury nature; he didn't bother to remove them even though it was a cloudy day.

Still, I admitted that I was indeed Henry's brother.

'Let's sit and have a chat,' said Rogga Lundberg. 'I know Henry. It would be fun to get to know his brother, too. Who's your mate?'

'Edmund,' said Edmund.

We reluctantly sat down at the garden table. Rogga lit a cigarette.

'I've worked with Henry,' he said. 'At *Kurren*. I'm freelance, too.'

The word 'freelance' suddenly lost some of its sheen.

'So, things have happened here.' He gestured meaningfully toward the woods and the clearing. Edmund and I didn't move a muscle.

'It's not every day that there's a murder on our doorstep. Yup, I'm doing a little writing about it, you know. One man's death is another man's bread. You read *Kurren*, don't you?'

'We don't know anything about it,' I said.

'We just happen to live nearby,' said Edmund.

'Really?' said Rogga Lundberg and smiled briefly. 'But I think Henry knows a lot, doesn't he?'

'What's that supposed to mean?' I said.

He didn't answer right away. He clasped his hands behind his neck and leaned back in the chair as if he were sunning himself. Wearing those bloody sunglasses. Even though it was cloudy. He took two drags from his cigarette and then let it hang from the corner of his mouth.

'When's he back, did you say?'

'Late,' I said, suddenly reminded of the conversation I'd had with Berra Albertsson just under a week ago. It had been almost exactly like this, and it felt so uncanny that the hairs on the back of my neck stood up. 'Won't be back until tonight, probably.'

'Does he have nocturnal habits, your brother?'

I didn't answer. Edmund took off his glasses and rubbed the bridge of his nose. I knew this was a nervous tic.

'Listen,' said Rogga Lundberg in a serious tone. 'It's just as well that you understand what the police are thinking. Or that Henry does. That's why I want to have a chat with him.'

'Is that so?' I said.

He flicked his cigarette over his shoulder. 'It's not that strange,' he said. 'Clever lads like you shouldn't have a hard time catching my drift. Especially if you put your heads together.'

We didn't reply.

'Berra Albertsson was found up where you park the cars. Right? On the night between Wednesday and Thursday last week?'

I nodded reluctantly.

'Someone killed him just as he was getting out of his car. So, the police's first conclusion must be that he'd intended to park there. Can you tell me why?'

'You don't have to answer,' Rogga Lundberg continued when neither Edmund nor I showed any sign of wanting to speak. 'It's obvious. There is only one reason you'd park up there. Either he was going to visit the Lundins or he was going to visit you … Either-or. There are no other alternatives. What do you have to say about that?'

'Maybe he was stopping for a piss,' said Edmund.

'And a madman just happened to be up there,' I said.

Rogga Lundberg didn't mind the interruption.

'Let me tell you, the police were working from this premise from the start: that Super-Berra had planned on coming here—or going to the Lundins' over there …' He nodded nonchalantly toward the Lundins'. 'And there was someone who wanted to prevent him from getting there. Or here. And who succeeded … Hmm?'

The question mark after the 'hmm' was as clear as anything, but neither I nor Edmund made any attempt to reply.

'The police focused on the Lundins first, of course—they're no strangers to this sort of thing. Unfortunately that didn't lead anywhere. There's not much pointing to their involvement this time around.'

'How c-c-could you know that?' said Edmund. 'Y-y-you're talking bollocks.'

It was the first time that I'd heard Edmund stutter. Rogga Lundberg lost track of himself for a moment. Then he sniffed contemptuously and took out another cigarette.

'This is what I need to talk to Henry about,' he said. 'Shame he isn't home. It'll be too bad if we can't have a chat soon.'

Cancer-Treblinka-Love-Fuck-Death, I thought for the first time in a long time.

'So you should probably tell him I stopped by and tell him what I said. You can say that I know about his romantic entanglements, too. One in particular. He'll understand.'

He got up and lit a cigarette, looking at us through his dark lenses. Then he shrugged and left.

We stayed put for a long time and tried to put him out of our minds. But we couldn't.

It was probably the conversation with Rogga Lundberg that made us tackle the Ewa Kaludis problem that very Wednesday.

Henry was sleeping when we got up. We hadn't heard him come home the previous night, and before we set off, we left a note on the kitchen table saying that a colleague had come looking for him. I didn't want to write anything else; it would be better to tell him the rest when we were back in the evening.

It was a warm but windy day. We left on our bikes in the morning, but Edmund got a puncture about halfway between Sjölycke and Åsbro. We had to go down into civilization and spend an hour outside of Laxman's with a bucket of water, patches and rubber solution. Britt Laxman wasn't there; Edmund and I thought that was just as well, and finally we decided that the inner tube would be able to hold air again.

The headwind meant that we didn't reach town until around two. We'd called my dad from Laxman's—it was the second of his three weeks of holiday and he hadn't yet gone to the hospital—and said that we were thinking of stopping by Idrottsgatan. When we arrived, he had just started to prepare mince patties with onions.

His cooking was so-so, as usual, but we were hungry and he looked pleased when we were done.

'Good, boys. Eat until you burst. You never know when you're going to get your next meal.'

'Truer words were never spoken,' said Edmund.

'Has it settled down out there?' my father asked.

We nodded. If we let anything slip about Henry and Ewa Kaludis or about Rogga Lundberg, then he'd lock us in on the spot and forbid us from setting foot in Gennesaret ever again. I realized that I felt ashamed of keeping him in the dark and hoped that somehow I'd have a chance to explain everything afterward.

Somehow. I just didn't know how.

'It's good that you have each other, boys,' said my father.

'A burden shared is a burden halved,' said Edmund.

We ate rhubarb cream for pudding; my father wondered if

163

I felt like coming along to see my mother, but I explained that Edmund and I had some things to take care of. He was fine with that, and we all left Idrottsgatan together.

My father, to catch the bus to Örebro. Us, to pay a visit to the fiancée whom the murdered handball star had left behind.

But first we procrastinated for two hours.

We spent the first in the culvert and smoked the four loose Ritzes that we'd bought at the kiosk at the station when we passed through Hallsberg.

The second we spent sitting on a bench in Brandstationsparken fifty metres from the yellow-tiled villa on Hambergsgatan.

We weren't really sure what we wanted to talk to Ewa Kaludis about. The closer we came to the moment we'd be face-to-face with her, the colder our feet got. We didn't seem to want to admit it to each other, but I saw that Edmund was at least as jittery about seeing her again as I was.

Because Ewa Kaludis might be keeping a lot to herself. She might know things that maybe it was better for two fourteen-year-old admirers not to know.

On the other hand, she might very well need our help; that was why we had embarked on this gentlemanly relief mission. When all was said and done, there was nothing to suggest that she and my brother Henry had had any contact with each other in the week since the murder—at least, that's what we thought after looking at the situation forward, backward and sideways.

Neither of us wanted to come to a definite conclusion.

On the other-other hand (and maybe this was what gave us our courage) there was a good chance that she wouldn't be home at all on a day like this, and that we could return to Gennesaret with our self-esteem intact and our task unaccomplished.

When the Emmanuel Church's clock struck half five, Edmund sighed deeply.

'Sod it,' he said. 'We're going to ring her bell. Now.'

And so we did.

18

'Erik and Edmund,' Ewa Kaludis exclaimed. 'So good of you to come. It's been … no, actually, I don't know.'

We could hardly comprehend that we were actually inside Ewa Kaludis's home. And that she lived in this gleaming tiled mansion. She and Super-Berra; well, Super-Berra didn't live here any more, but you could definitely feel his presence. Framed diplomas hung on the walls and most of the shelves of the large bookcase in the living room were filled with trophies and plaques that testified to what an outstanding athlete he'd been. The coolest one hung above the TV. A huge photograph of Berra Albertsson shaking hands with Ingemar Johansson. They both wore ties and were giving the camera crooked and world-weary smiles, so you could tell beyond a shadow of a doubt that these weren't just any old nobodies. I felt a little ill when I looked at the picture; it sort of flickered inside my head.

Otherwise, Ewa was clearly happy that we were there. She seemed to have been expecting us. When we'd finished staring at the trophies she led us straight through the house to the back patio where there was a table with a parasol and four chairs. She invited us to sit and asked if we wanted squash and cake.

We did, and she disappeared inside the house again.

'What a pad,' said Edmund.

'Mm,' I said.

'Did you see Ingo?'

I nodded. Then we sat in silence and held on to the sun-warmed armrests, which were made of a fragrant, dark brown wood, trying to adapt to our surroundings. It wasn't easy. Certainly none of my friends' houses, at least the ones that I had visited, had been anything like this, and the tingling in my body and Edmund's grew stronger the longer we sat, waiting, feeling small. I peered furtively through the balcony door. It was remarkable. Large expanses of floor without any furniture. No specific function. A glass table. A tree in a huge clay pot. An odd painting with triangles and circles in red and blue. Bloody remarkable, actually.

And it all looked as though it had been picked up from the furniture factory last week. I glanced at Edmund and saw that he was having similar thoughts. This place was something else. Berra and Ewa Kaludis were of a different species, and I felt dispirited. As if the distance between myself and Ewa was once again insurmountable.

As if it ever could have been surmountable.

I'm not sure what I meant by that. My thoughts wandered and spun, and I bit my cheek and decided I was a self-involved git, sitting here thinking these daft thoughts. Circumstances being what they were.

Ewa returned with a tray that held a jug, glasses and a small plate with pieces of chocolate hedgehog slice.

'So good of you to have come,' she repeated and sat across from us. 'I've been so worried … didn't know what I … what I should do.'

She still had traces of his fists on her face. Around her eye it was yellowish with patches of blue and her lower lip was swollen and still bore the scab.

'Well, we thought ...' said Edmund. '... that we'd pop by. While we were in town anyway.'

'And hear how you've been,' I added.

Ewa poured the yellow squash for us.

'It's ... I don't understand it,' she said.

I wondered what it was she didn't understand, but I didn't say anything.

'We're sorry for your loss,' said Edmund.

Ewa looked at him with surprise, as though she hadn't quite understood what he'd said.

'Loss?' she said. 'Oh, that, of course.'

I reached over and took a piece of hedgehog slice. I wondered if she had made it herself. And if so, had she done it before or after the murder? It tasted pretty fresh, but I assumed that they had a freezer, so it could be either-or.

'Have you seen Henry lately?' I asked.

She shook her head.

'Not since ... No, not since.'

'Oh?' said Edmund. 'No, that's probably just as well.'

Ewa sighed deeply, and it was only then that I realized just how worried she was. When I dared to look at her more closely I saw that her eyes were bloodshot, and I guessed that she'd been crying. Fairly recently, too.

'Does he know?' she asked. 'Does Henry know you're here?'

'No,' Edmund and I said simultaneously.

'Hm,' said Ewa Kaludis, and I couldn't tell if she thought it was for better or worse that Henry hadn't sent us.

Maybe she'd been hoping that we had a message from him, maybe not. There was a pause while we ate cake and drank squash.

'It wasn't good between us,' she said. 'It wasn't good between me and Berra. You must be wondering.'

'Well,' said Edmund.

I said nothing and tied a shoelace that had come undone.

'It couldn't have carried on, but it didn't have to end this way. I feel sorry for Henry; it's all my fault. If I'd only known … even in my wildest imagination, I couldn't have pictured this …'

'There's so little we can be certain of,' I said.

'Man proposes but God disposes,' said Edmund.

'I don't know how I didn't see Bertil for who he was until it was too late,' Ewa continued. 'How could I not have known it was wrong from the start? When I met your brother, I realized how mad it all was. Dear God, if some things could be undone.' She paused and ran her fingers over her swollen lip. 'Still, I did love him once. If only you could turn back the clock, just one time.'

I saw that she was talking more to herself now than to Edmund and me. Her words weren't meant for the ears of fourteen-year-old boys, I could tell, and while I was thinking that, I also felt sorry for Berra Albertsson.

Apart from him being dead, that is.

It couldn't have been much fun to be loved by a woman like Ewa Kaludis and then wake up one morning to find that love gone.

Even though this only flew through my mind in a split second, I suspected it was one of the few truly deep thoughts I'd had lately.

One of those questions that need to be revisited.

If it's better to be loved and then unloved, or not to be subjected to it in the first place.

169

That's the 'clincher', as I think they say.

'I wander around here not knowing which way is which,' said Ewa Kaludis. 'I'm sorry I'm talking to you like this, I'm not myself.'

'We understand,' said Edmund. 'Sometimes you're really stuck in the muck, and you don't know how to get out.'

Ewa didn't answer. I cleared my throat and plucked up the courage.

'Were you there that night?' I asked.

She took a deep breath and looked at me.

'In Gennesaret?' I clarified.

She looked at Edmund and then she answered.

'Yes,' she said. 'I was there.'

'Do the police know?' I asked.

She leaned back in the chair and folded her hands in her lap.

'No,' she said. 'The police don't know anything about Henry and me.'

'Good,' said Edmund.

'At least I think they don't,' Ewa added. 'But send my regards to Henry, will you? Give him a message from me?'

'Of course,' I said. 'What should we tell him?'

She thought for a moment.

'Tell him,' she said. 'Tell him that everything will be fine and he shouldn't worry on my behalf.'

I didn't think this was how she was really feeling, but I still committed it to memory.

Word for word, her message to Henry, my brother.

Everything will be fine and you shouldn't worry on Ewa Kaludis's behalf.

Before we left, she hugged both of us. Her bare arms and shoulders were warm from the sun and I found the courage to hug her back properly. I took a long sniff and breathed in the scent of her skin, and a cloud of Ewa Kaludis unfurled in my head.

It felt fantastic. The swelling cloud suffused me and held the Incident and Cancer-Treblinka and everything else unpleasant at bay for a few hours. Only when we rode past Laxman's did the cloud dissipate. It was immediately replaced by a cold emptiness in my stomach.

As though it was gripped by an icy fist.

So, maybe, I thought, maybe it would have been best not to inhale Ewa Kaludis.

Maybe it would be easier to sit on the loo for the rest of my life and forget about putting myself out there. Maybe Edmund's theory about the soul wasn't so crazy after all. It was easy to find, if you could be bothered to pay attention and try to feel for it.

Here, on this rough potholed path between Åsbro and Sjölycke, my soul was at the centre of my heart.

It seemed to travel to where it hurt the most. Who knew why.

Henry still hadn't returned when we arrived back at Gennesaret, and that was just as well. I'd have to have a serious talk with him, both about what Rogga Lundberg had said and about our visit to Ewa, but for the moment—in the fatal emptiness beyond that fragrant cloud—I was so downhearted that I couldn't face it.

Edmund wasn't in much better spirits. We ate a few bland hot dogs with bread—no mustard because there wasn't any left—took a quick dip off the dock and went to bed.

'This doesn't feel good, Erik,' said Edmund when we had turned off the light. 'How could a brilliant summer like this one go so wrong? So goddamn wrong.'

'Let's sleep on it,' I said.

19

'Let's take the boat out,' said my brother Henry, and so we did.

Henry rowed and I sat on the thwart. It was another sunny day with a lot of wind; we approached the waves aslant en route to Seagull Shit Island. Henry missed a stroke now and again and I realized I was actually a much better oarsman than he was. He insisted on smoking while he rowed, which of course made it much harder for him. When we were about one hundred metres from the island, he lifted the oars out of the water and took off his short-sleeved sweater.

'We need to have a chat,' he said.

'Yes,' I said. 'I suppose we do.'

'I didn't know it would turn out this way.'

'Neither did I.'

He lit two Lucky Strikes and handed one to me.

'Like I said, no idea.'

I nodded.

'What did Rogga Lundberg want?'

I told him about the conversation with Rogga Lundberg and while I talked Henry was running his hand over his stubble and looked even more sombre. When I finished he sat in silence for a spell, staring out at Fläskhällen, where we were slowly drifting.

'Would you say his behaviour was threatening?' he asked.

I thought about it.

'Yes,' I said. 'I thought so. I think he only wanted to take advantage of you somehow.'

'Good,' said Henry. 'Good on you, brother. You can already read people. That's not bad for your age; most people never learn. Rogga Lundberg is an asshole. Always has been.'

'Like Berra Albertsson?'

Henry laughed.

'Not quite. A different kind. There are many types of asshole, and the trick is to know what kind you're dealing with.'

I nodded. Henry fell silent again. I leaned over the edge of the boat and caught a wave with my hand. I rinsed my face. Henry watched me and then did the same. It wasn't much, but I felt more equal to him than ever before. I cleared my throat and looked away. I knew I was blushing.

Henry drummed his fingers on his knee.

'Anything else?' he asked.

'We visited Ewa yesterday.'

For a moment, he looked quite surprised.

'Oh?'

'She sent a message.'

He raised an inquisitive brow.

'We were supposed to tell you that everything will be fine and you don't have to worry on her behalf.'

Henry nodded and sank back into his thoughts. Then he cleared his throat and spat in the water.

'That's good,' he said. 'It was nice of you to visit her.'

I wondered if I should tell him that she had seemed worried, but I decided not to. No need to add to his burden. Sufficient unto the day is the evil thereof.

'Well, that settles it,' said Henry after another silence.

'What do you mean?' I said.

'Rogga Lundberg,' said Henry. 'If Rogga knows about Ewa and me, then the police probably ought to know, too.'

'I was thinking of suggesting that,' I said, because I had been.

'There's no reason to put your destiny in the hands of someone like him. Remember that, brother. When you have to tell the truth, you have to. There are no shortcuts, and you have to do it yourself. Do you know where I was yesterday?'

I shook my head. 'No.'

'With the police.' He laughed his short, sharp laugh. 'I spent the whole afternoon at the police station in Örebro with Detective Superintendent Lindström and two other detectives. They couldn't agree on whether to let me go or not, but in the end Lindström decided that I could. But I'm barred from travelling.'

'A travel ban? How does that work?'

Henry shrugged.

'I can't go off anywhere, have to stay close to home ... So, it's just as well that I talk to them about Ewa.'

I thought about it.

'Before they find out from someone else,' I said.

'Exactly,' said Henry and splashed a fresh handful of water on his face. 'Before some asshole or other tries to earn a few bob. I wonder if that bastard's been to see Ewa as well.'

'She didn't say anything,' I said.

'No,' said Henry. 'Let's hope that he hasn't had the chance.'

He took hold of the oars again. A few seagulls came flying our way, shrieking. Henry cursed at them; then he took a long, serious look at me before he began to row.

'I don't like talking about this,' he said. 'And I know that you don't either. But it had to be done. Do you think we know where we stand now?'

'I think so,' I answered.

Before Henry set off he gave me and Edmund seventy kronor for the shopping. Every last cheese rind in the larder had been eaten, so we were sorely in need of provisions. On top of that, once Henry was at the police station, he might not return to Gennesaret—if they'd been unsure of him yesterday, then he'd hardly be better off after admitting to having relations with the deceased's fiancée.

It was just like a Perry Mason story, Edmund and I concurred, when I told him about the conversation.

Except that Perry himself was nowhere to be found.

We took the bikes out that day, spent every last sausage-coin at Laxman's and on the way back Edmund told me more about his real dad.

About how he used to cry.

'Cry?' I said. 'What do you mean, cry?'

'When he was hitting me,' said Edmund. 'Or after. When he was done. Sometimes, anyway.'

'Why did he cry?'

'I don't know,' said Edmund. 'I've never understood it. He would sit on his bed and whimper and say that it hurt him more than it hurt me, and that I'd understand when I was older.'

'What were you supposed to understand?'

Edmund shrugged so sharply that he lost his balance and almost fell over his handlebars. He regained control of the bike and swore. 'How the hell should I know? Why he had to beat me up, I suppose. As if there was a reason, but that I was too young to understand … that he was hitting me against his will somehow. As if something were forcing him to and he couldn't resist it …'

We pedalled in silence.

'Why would you hit somebody on purpose and then cry about it?' I said. 'That's strange.'

'He was sick,' said Edmund. 'There's no other explanation. Sick from worms crawling around and eating up his brain or something like that.'

'That sounds like a load of nonsense,' I said, but deep inside—deep down in an underdeveloped part of my fourteen-year-old brain—I suspected that people like that did in fact exist.

People who cried over what they did and those to whom they did it.

I didn't like it. This idea directly contradicted what Henry and I had talked about.

When you have to tell the truth, you have to.

No, I had no desire to think about Edmund's dad and his sort. As I said, I had decided that long before. Cancer-Treblin-ka-Love-Fuck-Death.

No further questions.

20

My brother Henry was charged with the murder of Bertil 'Berra' Albertsson on Thursday 19 July, and it was in the papers on Friday.

It was also on that Friday that Edmund and I received another visit from Detective Superintendent Verner Lindström. He had arrived by nine in the morning, and had brought a few copies of the *Läns* newspaper with him. First he had us read about developments in the case, and then he interrogated us.

Henry wasn't named, he was either called 'the accused' or 'the suspect' and it wasn't mentioned that he had gone to the police of his own volition.

And neither was there anything about what had made him a suspect in the first place. All the reports said was that the suspect had had 'certain relations' with the victim. The charge was the result of a laborious and fruitful investigation, but the young man hadn't confessed to anything, Detective Lindström had said during a short press conference on Thursday evening.

There was no more to it.

'False information has been given about this case,' Lindström said when we'd finished reading. 'By you two, for instance. This time I want the truth, gentlemen. The whole truth.'

He sounded much rougher than before. Like sandpaper.

Edmund folded the newspaper and pushed it back across the table.

'And nothing but the truth,' he said in English.

'Wait outside for now,' said Lindström. 'Stay close. And stick to Swedish from here on in.'

Edmund's cheeks went a little red, and he left us alone in the kitchen.

Lindström took out the tube of Bronzol but didn't open it. He just placed it on the table and rolled it back and forth with the index and middle fingers of his right hand. Apparently, he didn't need a notebook this time around; I didn't really know how I was supposed to interpret that.

I didn't know how I was supposed to interpret the silence either, the one he filled with the sound of his breath flowing in and out of his hairy nostrils while he watched me, no more than an arm's length away. He was like a cold sun lamp; I alternated between staring at the Bronzol and my hands, which I wrung in my lap.

'You and your brother,' he finally began.

'Yes?' I said.

'What's it like between you two?'

'Good,' I said.

'He's quite a bit older than you.'

That didn't sound like a question, so I didn't answer.

'How much older?'

'Just over eight years.'

'Would you say you know him well?'

'Oh yes,' I said.

'You know what he gets up to and so forth?'

'Oh yes.'

'What does he do?'

'Journalism,' I said. 'He's freelance. But he's taken time off this summer to write a book.'

'A book?'

'Yes.'

'What kind of book?'

'A novel,' I said. 'About life.'

'Life?'

'Yes.'

Lindström tapped the tube on the table, but still he didn't open it.

'How does he do with the ladies?'

I shrugged and looked disinterested.

'Well, I suppose.'

'Who's Emmy Kaskel?'

'Emmy? His ex-fiancée.'

'Ex?'

'Yes.'

'And who's his fiancée now?'

I looked at his blue polka-dot bow tie. Had it been a Christmas present from his wife? Did he even have a wife?

'No one, I think.'

'Really?'

I didn't answer.

'How does Ewa Kaludis fit in, then?'

'She was our supply teacher this spring,' I said.

'I know she was your supply teacher,' said Lindström. 'You told me last time. Now I want to know what kind of relationship she had with your brother Henry.'

'I think they know each other,' I said.

'Aha,' said Lindström. 'You think they know each other. How come you didn't tell me this last time?'

'You didn't ask,' I said.

He paused and his breathing filled the silence again as he studied the fingers on his left hand, as though he were checking for dirt under his nails.

'How old did you say you were?'

'I didn't.'

'So tell me.'

'Fourteen.'

'Fourteen? Only fourteen years old, and you think you need to protect your twenty-two-year-old brother?'

'I'm not trying to protect my brother. I don't know what you mean.'

Lindström screwed up his mouth.

'You know very well what I mean,' he said. 'You've always known that Henry was involved with Ewa Kaludis, and you think that you're helping him by keeping that to yourself.'

'That's not how it is,' I said.

Lindström ignored my interjection. He was on a roll, and it was starting to feel like a cross-examination.

'You think that you're helping Henry by keeping some things to yourself,' he explained. 'That's not correct. You're on the wrong tack, just like your friend. Henry has told us everything and having his little brother try to pull the wool over our eyes only hurts him.'

'I said that they knew each other.'

He opened the tube and tossed two pastilles into his mouth.

'How many times has she been here?'

I shrugged again.

'A couple. Three, maybe.'

'At what time?'

'I don't remember. Nights, I think.'

'Nights?'

'Maybe.'

'This July?'

I thought about it.

'Yes, maybe.'

He leaned back and looked out of the window. He seemed tired all of a sudden. I guessed that he hadn't slept much lately. He probably had a lot on his plate. He chewed the pastilles. Then he continued.

'So Ewa Kaludis spent a couple or more nights here in the house with your brother Henry at the beginning of July. Are we in agreement on that point?'

I nodded softly.

'You knew that Ewa Kaludis was Bertil Albertsson's fiancée?'

'Yes.'

'Didn't you think it was strange that she was sleeping here with your brother instead of with her fiancé?'

'I didn't think about it much.'

He studied the nails on his other hand.

'The eleventh of July,' he then said. 'Tell me about the eleventh of July.'

'What day was it?' I asked.

'Wednesday last week. The day before the night that Bertil Albertsson was murdered.'

I thought a good while.

'I don't really remember,' I said. 'It wasn't anything special, I think.'

'You remembered it well the last time we spoke.'

'I did?'

His fist slammed on the table. It was like a gunshot. I flinched and almost fell backward out of my chair. I caught myself on the table top at the last second and recovered my balance.

'Enough mucking about,' Lindström snapped, his voice coarser than sandpaper now. 'We know that Henry had Ewa Kaludis over that night, and we know that you know. If you want to make things the tiniest bit easier on your brother, you have to tell us what happened. Everything you're holding back. The way you're going, you're making it worse for him.'

I didn't reply right away. I counted backward from ten to zero and avoided looking at him.

'You're wrong,' I said. 'I have no idea if Ewa Kaludis was here that night. We fell asleep early, both Edmund and I, and I didn't wake once during the night.'

Detective Lindström put the Bronzol tube in his jacket's inner pocket. Buttoned all three buttons and put his elbows on the table. I met his gaze. Five seconds passed. I aged ten years.

'Go and get your friend,' said Lindström.

After I had taken two steps out on to the lawn, he changed his mind.

'Stop!' he called. 'I'll get him myself.'

'Of course, detective,' I said and walked toward the lake.

Edmund looked downhearted when he came and lay beside me on the dock half an hour later.

'Has he gone?' I asked.

Edmund nodded.

'It's bloody awful,' he said. 'They're thinking of locking him up for it.'

'He'll be fine,' I said.

'You think?' said Edmund.

'Henry always comes out on top.'

'I hope you're right,' said Edmund.

We lay in silence. It'd been a cloudy morning, but now the

sun was breaking through and it was getting warmer. The dock swayed slowly and the waves lapped against it.

I wondered what Detective Lindström had asked Edmund about, and what Edmund had said, but I didn't want to talk about it.

'Should we take a trip to Seagull Shit Island?' I asked instead. 'While we still can.'

Edmund sat up and dipped his feet in the water.

'Yes,' he said. 'Let's. They're going to collect us any minute now, don't you think?'

'Probably,' I said. 'It probably won't be long.'

Edmund sighed and squinted at the lake.

'One last boat trip,' he said. 'It's just too sad. It was such a damn good summer.'

'It was,' I said. 'Yes, it was.'

Our fathers were waiting for us as we rowed back. They had been there for over an hour and our things were out on the lawn, packed and ready to go.

'You're coming with us,' said my father. 'It's enough now.'

Albin Wester said nothing, and it looked as though he had sold all the prisoners at the Grey Giant and then lost the money. Edmund and I changed into our clothes and ten minutes later we left Gennesaret. This time my dad had borrowed an old Citroën from the Bergmans, who lived two houses down on Idrottsgatan. It was rusty and knackered, and even though it was only twenty-five kilometres to town, we had to stop twice because the water in the radiator was boiling.

'We could have taken our bikes,' said Edmund.

'We'll get the bikes later,' Edmund's dad said crossly. 'You know there are more important things to think about right now, don't you?'

'French cars aren't built for the Swedish summer heat,' said my father. Then he burned himself on the radiator cap.

21

The days after Henry was taken into custody were strange. Although the world was topsy-turvy and it felt like all sorts of things were happening, it was still monotonous.

Almost every day my father and I drove Killer into Örebro. First we visited Henry at the police station, then my mother at the hospital. The very fact that my father, not Henry, was driving Killer was a sure sign that things were off-kilter. My father probably didn't fit in anywhere, but he stuck out like a sore thumb behind the wheel of the black VW. Under normal circumstances, he was a terrible driver; in Killer his driving was catastrophic; more than once I thought: 'Here it comes', and, 'The last thing we need now is a car accident. On top of everything else.'

Still, we got through each day with our skin intact. Off to Örebro in the morning and back again in the evening. Neither of us had much to say when we visited Henry in his pale yellow cell in the basement of the police station, not me nor my father nor my brother. There was a bed attached to the wall, a small table, two chairs and a lamp. Henry usually lay on his bed, while my father and I sat on the chairs. Every day my father brought a copy of *Kurren* with him and a pack of Lucky Strikes and every day Henry had a hole in his sock close to his right big toe. I started to wonder if he ever changed his socks, but I didn't want to ask.

'How can they be allowed to treat honest people this way? They should be ashamed of themselves,' my father would say.

Or: 'This time tomorrow, you'll be out of here, you'll see.'

Henry rarely commented. Usually he'd start reading *Kurren* as soon as we'd sat down, smoking ardently, as if he'd gone without cigarettes for days.

After our visit to the slammer, we'd go to the bakery. Three Roses or New Pomona on Rudbecksgatan. My father would drink coffee with his cinnamon bun, I'd have a Pommac and a rosette or a Pommac and a Mazarin tart.

'I've taken some extra holiday,' my father would explain halfway through his cinnamon bun each day. 'I thought it was best until this sorts itself out.'

'It's been a difficult summer,' I would reply.

At the hospital everything was the same except for two things: my mother looked much worse, and my father had started to cry at her bedside.

When I saw it coming, I often made a point of going to the loo. It was quite a pleasant one—large and spacious. The walls were adorned with small not-quite-square tiles and while I sat there with my trousers and pants pushed down around my ankles, I tried to play noughts and crosses against myself in my head. It was very hard, considering the tiles weren't quite square, and I never really liked the idea of beating myself at the game.

'You're taking care of yourself, Erik?' my mother would ask before we left her.

'Yes, indeed,' I would often promise.

'Hold on to your courage,' she might say. 'It'll be too heavy to pick back up once you've dropped it.'

And then my father and I would nod earnestly.

Truer words were never spoken.

I think it was Wednesday when an 'R.L.' byline first appeared in conjunction with an article in *Kurren* about the Berra Albertsson murder.

He didn't name Henry, but he wrote about Gennesaret and about Ewa Kaludis, and that the perpetrator who was now in police custody in Örebro was most likely a former reporter for the newspaper. It also said that the motive behind the gruesome deed had been established and that it had been a so-called 'crime of passion'.

And that it was only a matter of time before Detective Lindström and his capable men would break down the accused and extract a confession.

A confession to his infamous deed.

As Henry read Rogga Lundberg's article, he laughed out loud several times, so hard that my father and I wondered if he was okay.

Was the pressure wearing him down? Was he going to crack, just as Rogga Lundberg had predicted?

'Pressure?' said Henry when my father asked him with a worried face about how he was doing. 'As if I'd take what that arch-cretin was writing seriously. What do you take me for? I thought we were related?'

I didn't know what an 'arch-cretin' was, but it was something of a relief to hear Henry talking like that.

It seemed my father thought so too, because that day he didn't cry at the hospital and in the car on the way home he said: 'What a lad, Erik. You can't keep him down.'

Soon after he said that, he overtook a car for the first time in five days.

Edmund and I met only one other time that summer: when Lasse Crook-mouth's dad had driven his Ford van to the town square to deliver our bikes the Sunday after we left Gennesaret. I asked Edmund if he wanted to come to Idrottsgatan for a bit, but he explained that he had to hurry home and pack. His dad had arranged for him to spend the rest of the holidays at his cousin's in Mora.

Edmund had told me about his cousins once when we rowed to Laxman's, and he'd described them as two deaf-mute bed-wetters with underbites. Now it seemed as though they had grown into themselves; Edmund said that he'd probably have quite a good time up there.

'They have rabbits and everything.'

'Rabbits?' I said.

'And everything,' said Edmund, fidgeting.

We said 'See you later' and wished each other luck.

About a week after Henry was taken into custody, my father and I went back to Gennesaret to pick up the rest of our bits and bobs. Clothes and groceries and so on. It was raining cats and dogs the entire time we were there and we stayed no longer than necessary. When my father looked through the shed, he noticed that the sledgehammer was missing. He called me over and asked if we had used it.

'Not that I recall,' I said. 'Maybe when we were building the dock?'

'Take a look around and see if you can find it,' said my father.

I went out in the rain and looked for it, then I explained that

I couldn't find it and I didn't know where it could have got to. My father had a strange look in his eyes, but he didn't say anything. He just stood there, staring at me as if he'd never seen anything like me before.

As if I were a jigsaw puzzle—yes, that's what came to mind as we stood in the kitchen at Gennesaret that rainy day. I was a jigsaw puzzle that my dad had been trying to solve my whole life and now he was getting close. Maybe all people were jigsaw puzzles to each other, and some of us were jigsaw puzzles to ourselves.

It didn't take much time. We locked up, jogged up the path to the parking spot with our luggage and our grocery bags, loaded them into Killer, and drove away. Somewhere around the halfway mark to Hallsberg, my father asked: 'You don't have to answer. You absolutely don't have to answer, but do you think he did it?'

I considered his question and said: 'How could you possibly think that your own son is a murderer?'

Henry's typewriter and his stack of typed pages were among the things we brought home from Gennesaret. That evening I counted the sheets of paper in the pile: there were eighty-five pages. There were quite a few strike-throughs and additions, made in biro. No wonder Brylle and the others at Stava School used to complain about my spidery scrawl; my brother, who was eight years older, had barely decipherable handwriting.

I wondered about the page that had been left in the typewriter, the one I'd read and committed to memory a few weeks earlier. The one about the body and the gravel road and the summer night. I leafed through the stack of paper three times without finding it. I tried to remember it word for word, but so much had happened since, it had fallen out of my head.

I only remembered that it had been beautiful. Beautiful, surprising and a little frightening.

The next day we brought both the Facit and the typescript to Henry, because he'd asked for them. And a new packet of typing paper. You could tell he was eager for us to leave so he could start writing.

I thought it was a good sign that he wanted to sit down and clatter on again.

That in spite of it all, there was hope.

One evening a few days later I ran into Ewa Kaludis. I had been at Törner's and bought the sausage special because my father didn't have the energy to cook, and I could have sworn that she was there waiting for me. It was right by Nilsson's Cycle and Sport on the corner of Mossbanegatan and Östra Drottninggatan, and as far as I knew she had no other reason to be standing there. No apparent reason, anyway.

'Hi, Erik,' she said.

'Hi,' I said, perking up.

She was wearing the Swanson shirt and those black slacks again. And the hairband. Her bruises were barely visible and I was struck once again by how terribly beautiful she was.

So beautiful it hurt. It was as if I had somehow managed to forget this.

'Where are you going?' she asked.

'Home,' I said.

'Are you in a rush or can we chat? We can walk your way.'

'Sure,' I said. 'I'm in no hurry.'

We started to walk along Mossbanegatan. Even though I was only fourteen years old I was as tall as she was, and I got it into my head that from a distance people might think we were a couple out for a stroll. A young man and his girlfriend. My head was spinning with this thought and because she was walking so close to me.

And because we'd gone quite a way before she said anything. Almost all the way to Snukke's old asbestos-ridden villa.

'I'm afraid,' she then said.

'Of what?' I asked.

'Of visiting Henry at the police station.'

'Why?' I said. 'It's not bad; I go every day.'

'It's not that. I wonder what the police would make of it.'

'I see,' I said. 'Well, I don't know what they're thinking.'

'Neither do I,' said Ewa. 'And I don't want them to get the wrong idea.'

I wondered what idea they'd get that they didn't already have. What could make this worse?

But I didn't ask what she meant.

'Would you give him this letter for me?' she asked when we'd almost reached Karlesson's shop.

I took the sealed envelope, which had neither a name nor an address written on it. All that distinguished it was that it was light blue.

Then we didn't say much else, but before we parted I plucked up the courage. An incredible courage. I don't know where it came from.

I stood before Ewa Kaludis. Our faces were no more than twenty centimetres apart. I reached out both of my hands and placed them on her upper arms.

'Ewa,' I said. 'I don't care that I'm only fourteen years old. You are the most beautiful woman on earth and I love you.'

She gasped.

'I had to say it,' I said. 'That's all. Thank you very much.'

Then I kissed her and walked away.

I dreamed of Ewa Kaludis for the rest of the summer. Images of her making love to my brother Henry came to me and sometimes I was the one who was lying there instead of Henry. Often I was in two places at once: both outside the window and underneath Ewa. Underneath her and inside her. When I woke in the mornings I couldn't always remember if I'd dreamed of her or not, but if I wanted to find out I just had to look at the sheets to see if there were new spots. More often than not there were.

Of course it wasn't easy keeping her out of my thoughts during the days either; I made a point of fantasizing about her while I was in the loo at the hospital. It was a good alternative to noughts and crosses, and sometimes I would think about her when we were in Killer on our way to Örebro.

I'm going to the slammer to see Henry, my brother. Then I'm going to visit my dying mother in the hospital and think about Ewa Kaludis and have a wank.

When I put it that way, I felt ashamed.

Orientation at Kumla County Junior Secondary School was on 27 August and it was the same day my brother was remanded in custody. I was in a class called I:3 B, had a head teacher called Gunvald who had a lisp, thirty-two new friends and twelve new teachers. I was subjected to a string of hitherto unknown subjects like physics, chemistry, German and morning assembly, and generally gained new perspectives on life.

One Friday, about a month into the school year, Henry turned up. He was waiting for me outside the school gates when we'd finished for the day. I walked out with a handful of classmates whom I didn't know very well, and they fell silent around me. Of course everyone knew who Henry was and his sudden appearance reminded them that I was the murderer's brother.

I went up to him. He was wearing sunglasses, an unbuttoned nylon shirt and had a Lucky Strike hanging from the corner of his mouth. He was the spitting image of Ricky Nelson. Or Rick.

'Hi, Henry,' I said.

'Hi, brother,' said Henry and smiled his crooked smile. 'How's it going?'

'Bloody great,' I said. 'Have they let you go?'

'Yep,' said Henry. 'It's over now.'

He put his arm around my shoulder. We walked across the street and climbed into Killer. My new friends stayed by the school gate and pretended that they'd just fallen out of the sky and didn't really know which way to go.

Henry fired up Killer and we drove away leaving a cloud of dust in our wake. I thought about what he'd said at the start of June.

Life should be like a butterfly on a summer's day.

The autumn was a bridge that led to new territory. I never quite got a foothold at KJCSS. Edmund also went there, but he was in another class and we didn't socialize. I didn't really socialize with anyone any more. Not with people I knew already and not with new people. Benny and I sat out in the culvert and chatted a few times, but it wasn't like before. We grew apart and it happened more quickly than I could comprehend.

Generally, I did all my homework and was quite the model

pupil, I think. I got an A-plus on my first German exam and an AB on my maths test. I finished *Colonel Darkin and the Mysterious Heiress*, but didn't start on another adventure. I read books, mostly English and American detective stories, and started listening to Radio Luxembourg. I dreamed about Ewa Kaludis but never saw her.

Every so often *Kurren* would run an article about the murder of Berra Albertsson and the police's efforts to find the perpetrator. One Saturday they ran a lengthy summary of the case with maps and Xs where the body had been found and all that, but no new clues or suspects were uncovered. The police kept working on the case and Detective Lindström spoke to the newspaper in optimistic terms, claiming that it was only a matter of time until the murderer would be behind bars.

I don't know if *Kurren*'s regular readers believed him. I certainly had my doubts.

Henry moved to Göteborg in early November and on 3 December, my mother died. My father had been at her side during her last ten days, but I couldn't cope.

The funeral was a week later in Kumla's church. For the first time in my life, I wore a suit. About twenty of us followed my mother to her final resting place: Henry, my father and I sat on the first pew in the church; behind us sat relatives, a few colleagues, Benny's mother and father and Mr. Wester.

I'd cried the whole night long, and in the church, I didn't have any tears left.

III

22

The following February, my father applied for a job at AB Slotts, and at Easter we moved to Uppsala. I was fourteen going on fifteen when I left my childhood home and arrived in the city of mustard and education. I started at Cathedral School among the children of senior lecturers and doctors, let my hair grow, got spots and a gramophone.

The first year we lived in a cramped two-room flat behind Östra station, and then we moved to Glimmervägen in Eriksberg, a newly built residential area. We had a two-bedroom apartment with a view of cliffs and forest from the balcony. My father livened up; his shifts at the mustard factory were difficult, but the atmosphere was more relaxed there than at the prison. He made a number of new friends at work, started playing bridge once a week and gingerly pursued a friendship with a widow in Salabacke. As for me, I soon fell in love with a dark-haired girl who lived in the building next to ours, and in the summer I turned sixteen I lost my virginity on a blanket in Hågadalen while listening to 'The House of the Rising Sun' on the transistor radio she'd brought along. I'm not sure if she was losing hers then too, but she said she was.

Henry continued living in Göteborg and was given increasingly secure employment at *Göteborgs-Posten*. Two years and two months after Berra Albertsson's murder, his debut novel

Coagulated Love was published by Norstedts. It was well received by both *Svenska Dagbladet* and *Dagens Nyheter*, and his own paper gave it a decent review, but Henry never wrote another book. I read *Coagulated Love* over the Christmas holidays that same year and once again a few years later, but I didn't get much out of it on either occasion. When my father died in 1976 I found his signed copy of the book among his possessions; all of the pages had been sliced open, but there was a grocery receipt used as a bookmark between pages eighteen and nineteen.

My aunt, the victim of the moose-based tragedy, died in the Dingle madhouse a few weeks before I graduated from college; we managed to sell Gennesaret at a decent price, and when I started studying philosophy in the autumn, I was able to move into my own one-and-a-half-room flat on Geijersgatan. By this time, my virginity was but a distant memory. Even though I didn't look as much like Rick Nelson as my brother, I still had good luck with the opposite sex; female students came and went and then there was one who stayed.

She was called Ellinor and by the start of the eighties we'd managed to bring three children into the world. At that point Geijersgatan was also but a memory. We bought a house in Norby among the bourgeoisie and the boxwood; I taught history and philosophy at a college, and when Ellinor wasn't at home raising our children, she was employed as a lab assistant at a pharmaceutical company out in the Boländer area.

One May evening in the mid-eighties *Expressen* ran a two-page article about unsolved murders in Sweden, with a focus on cases where the statute of limitations was running out in a year or so.

One of these was Bertil Albertsson's murder. We were sitting out in the garden, Ellinor and I, the lilacs were about to bloom, and for the first time I told her what had happened at Gennesaret. When I got going, I realized just how much it fascinated my wife, and I strove to dredge up as many memories as I could out of the well of time and forgetting. Leaving out the odd detail, of course—even though we had a completely open and uninhibited relationship, I still felt embarrassed when I recalled how Edmund and I had masturbated by the window while Henry and Ewa Kaludis were making love inside. For instance.

When I finished talking, my wife asked: 'And Edmund? How did it go for Edmund?'

I shrugged.

'I don't have the faintest idea, actually.'

My wife gave me a bewildered look and wrinkled her forehead in a way that usually signalled that I had exposed her to some sort of deep-seated male incomprehensibility. Again.

'My God,' she said. 'You mean you lost touch, just like that?'

'My mother died,' I pointed out. 'We moved.'

My wife took the newspaper and read through the summary of the murder again. Then she leaned back in the lounger and thought a while.

'We'll look him up,' she said. 'We'll look him up and invite him to dinner.'

'Like hell we will,' I said.

To my surprise, getting a hold of Edmund Wester was no problem. Personally, I didn't lift a finger in the search, but in early June, just before graduation, Ellinor told me that she had found him and that he was going to come and eat crayfish with us in August.

'You went behind my back,' I said. 'Admit it.'

'Of course, my eagle,' my wife answered. 'Sometimes foolish men need to be circumvented.'

'Where is he living?' I asked. 'How did you reach him?'

'It wasn't hard,' my wife explained. 'He's a vicar in Ånge.'

I couldn't help but smile. Norrland again.

'He sounded friendly and genuinely happy to hear from me. He thought it was about time that you met up again. You should have plenty to talk about, he said.'

'Really?' I said. 'Well, don't get your hopes up.'

'He's coming out this way in August anyhow,' said my wife. 'It'll be interesting to meet him, whatever happens. You know, I've never met anyone who knew you as a child.'

'You've met my father,' I pointed out. 'And Henry.'

My wife waved her index finger dismissively.

'They don't count,' she said. 'Your father is dead. And I've seen your brother three times.'

She had a point. My father had been dead for almost a decade by now, and I hadn't been in contact with Henry at all since he emigrated to Uruguay at the end of the seventies. The most recent Christmas card had arrived four years ago on Maundy Thursday.

During the first week of the summer holidays that year I spent most of my time reflecting on my childhood, and one warm, fragrant night I dreamed of Ewa Kaludis for the first time in twenty years. Oddly, it wasn't an erotic dream; it was filled with images and impressions from the day after she'd been beaten up and had sat in the sun lounger massaging my shoulders.

Anyway, I thought it was strange when I woke up. And a bit of a shame, but you don't get to choose your dreams, now do you?

Only a few weeks before Edmund's visit did I realize that if he'd joined the priesthood he must have studied in Uppsala. I didn't leave that university town for a long time after I first set foot in it, so we would have been near each other as adults, Edmund and I. At least for a few years. Had we ever crossed paths in town—when I was a student, perhaps? Why wouldn't we have recognized each other? I brought this up with my wife, but she said that a person can change a lot between the ages of fourteen and twenty and that it was the rule rather than the exception that you missed people in a crowd.

When Edmund Wester turned up I saw that she was dead right.

The gargantuan man with a dense beard standing on our steps when I opened the door reminded me as much of four-teen-year-old Edmund as a duck reminds me of a sparrow. I did some rough sums in my head and concluded that if his weight gain had followed a steady trajectory then he'd have put on about five kilos a year since I'd last seen him at school in Kumla. It wasn't just the beard that hid the clerical collar, but his double chins. His worn corduroy suit had room for another three to four years of growth at the same rate.

'Erik Wassman, I presume?' he said, hiding the bouquet for my wife behind his back.

'Edmund,' I said. 'You haven't changed one bit.'

The evening was more pleasant than I'd dared hope. In each of our professions, we'd learned to make both frivolous and serious small talk, and the crayfish were truly exquisite, since my wife had made her signature marinade. Our children behaved quite well and went to bed without much of a fuss. We drank beer and wine and schnapps and cognac, and any disappointment Ellinor might have felt about our reluctance to discuss the summer in Gennesaret eventually ebbed away.

It's not that we didn't mention Berra Albertsson and the murder, but both Edmund and I changed the subject when she brought it up. I remember how we'd kept the same distance when it was all going on, and realized how remarkably easy it was to pick up where you had left off with some people, even after such a long time.

If my wife hadn't raised the subject of a priest's vow of silence and crises of conscience, it would have been a wholly successful night. Unfortunately we were already in deep when I noticed that Edmund was troubled by the question.

We were well on to the coffee and cognac too, so maybe it wasn't odd that I had a momentary lapse in concentration.

'I've never understood it,' said my wife. 'What gives a priest the right to keep quiet about things that normal people can't? Things they'd be punished for if *they* kept them quiet?'

'It's not that simple,' said Edmund.

'It couldn't be any simpler,' said my wife. 'What kind of God keeps murderers and miscreants under his wing?'

'There is more than one law,' said Edmund. 'And more than one judge.'

'Isn't our legal system built on Christian ethics?' she insisted. 'Isn't the West built on a Christian system of values? Isn't that clause a construct that's ready for the scrap heap?'

Edmund sat quietly and scratched his beard and suddenly looked sombre. I prepared a change of topic, but wasn't quick enough.

'There are cases,' he said. 'There will always be situations where a person needs to get something off their chest ... We could never impose a vow of silence on everyone, but there have to be people who have taken one. There have to be options. Someone who listens; someone to whom you can turn and ask for his ear when you need to the most. Where your words are taken and sealed.'

'I don't understand it,' said my wife.

'It's a difficult question,' Edmund repeated. 'There have been moments when I've had my doubts.'

Soon thereafter he took his leave. We promised to keep in touch, but it was clear to all three of us that this was mostly a concession to custom.

After he left, my wife and I sat in our armchairs for a while.

'It has something to do with the Gennesaret murder,' she said suddenly. She poured a finger of cognac for each of us.

'What do you mean?' I said. 'No more cognac for me.'

'The crisis of conscience, of course. His discomfort with the question. It's related to the murder of Berra Albertsson twenty years ago.'

'Twenty-three,' I said. 'Oh, nonsense.'

'It has nothing to do with being part of the clergy.'

'How much have you had to drink?' I asked. 'Of course something's happened to him. Someone confessed to a crime and he feels he can't go to the police. Every priest is bound to face that conflict at some point. It wasn't particularly polite of you to bring it up.'

My wife sipped her cognac pensively.

'All right,' she said. 'It was rude of me, but I still think I'm right. He's very nice, anyway.'

'I liked him then,' I said.

For about a week I was preoccupied by what had been said and what was left unspoken between Edmund, my wife and me. I finally called him in Ånge and got straight to the point.

'You know what happened that night, don't you?'

'Whatever do you mean?' Edmund asked indignantly.

'I mean, when you went out for a piss, for instance. That wasn't all, was it?'

There was a pause. The line crackled and, for a moment, I thought it might be Edmund's thought processes materializing in the bad connection.

'I have no reason to discuss this further with you,' he said finally. 'But I'd like to ask you the same question, if you don't mind. Do you know who killed Berra Albertsson?'

'How should I know?' I answered crossly. 'I was asleep, you know that perfectly well.'

We both sat in silence for a while at our ends of the line, and then we hung up.

Perhaps you could describe running into Ewa Kaludis that same autumn as an event that looked like a fantasy.

During a conference about educational materials, I stayed at a hotel in Göteborg for two nights, and if I'd had a hard time recognizing Edmund after several decades, I had no problem recognizing Ewa. No problem at all.

She was standing behind the reception desk when I checked in, and time didn't seem to have touched her. Same beautiful posture. Same high cheekbones. Same crescent eyes. Her blond hair was now red, a hue that suited her even better—I imagined it was her natural colour. Though she was surely approaching fifty, she was still an astonishing beauty.

At least in my opinion.

'Dear God.' The words slipped from me. 'Ewa Kaludis.'

She looked at the list of reservations.

'Aha, you've arrived,' she said. 'Yes, I saw your name.'

Ellinor and I had been unswervingly faithful since we'd been married, but I knew that in less than a minute, I'd crack. It wasn't just because I wanted to, but because—more importantly—I could tell Ewa wanted it, too. She called into the reception area and ordered a young blonde girl to take her place at the desk; she clearly held some sort of managerial position at the hotel. Then she flipped up the counter and walked over to me.

'I'll show you to your room,' she said. 'What fun to see you again after all these years.'

We rode the lift up.

'Do you remember the last thing you said to me that summer?' she asked when we were in the room.

I nodded.

'And what you did?'

I nodded again.

'Do you still have that fourteen-year-old inside of you?'

'Every single inch of him,' I answered.

She'd just had her period—and was a bit preoccupied—so on the first night we just talked.

'I want to thank you for what you did that summer,' said Ewa. 'Thank you and Edmund for how you acted afterward and whatnot. There was never really the right moment to say it.'

'I loved you,' I explained. 'I think Edmund loved you, too.'

She smiled.

'It was Henry who loved me. And I who loved Henry.'

I asked how it had gone between her and my brother. If anything had happened in the end, or if it had all run out with the sand after the Incident.

'We did meet up eventually,' she said after a pause. 'Here in Göteborg. More than a year later. We didn't dare before. Then we were together for a while. Did he never tell you?'

I shook my head.

'I've barely had any contact with my brother. He moved and we moved.'

'It never really worked,' she continued. 'I don't know why, but what happened, well, it was in the way. The Incident, as you call it.'

I nodded. I understood. I could see how it would've been odd if it had worked out. I hadn't thought about it that way when I was fourteen, sitting across from Detective Lindström, but now it seemed logical.

Not only that it hadn't lasted between Henry and Ewa, but that there was a reason for it.

A kind of justice.

'Are you married?' I asked.

She shook her head.

'Was. I have a fourteen-year-old daughter. That's why I don't have much time tonight.'

'I remember your hands on my shoulders,' I said. 'And I want to make love to you tomorrow night. To try at least.'

She laughed.

'I have time tomorrow,' she agreed. 'I'll try to meet your expectations, otherwise I think it will be enough to be able to sleep together.'

Sleeping wasn't enough. The night between 16 and 17 October I made love to Ewa Kaludis after waiting for over twenty years.

Making love to her for the first time was the most serious undertaking of my life, and I think that Ewa felt the same. Over the following year we met up a fair number of times—at ever more frequent intervals—and one month after the divorce with Ellinor came through, I moved to Göteborg. I managed to secure a decent job at a college out in Mölndal and by early 1987 we were living under the same roof.

Me, Ewa Kaludis and her daughter Karla.

'It feels like coming home,' I told Ewa that first night.

'Welcome home,' said Ewa.

Not many weeks passed before I had to tell her how Edmund and I had stood and watched while she made love with Henry that night. I'd only been an immature fourteen-year-old at the time, so I hoped she'd understand.

When I had finished the story she put her hand over her mouth and wouldn't look at me. At first I was worried, but then I noticed that she was laughing.

'What's going on with you?' I asked.

She grew serious, lowered her hand and took a deep breath.

'I saw you,' she said. 'I didn't want to say, but I knew all along that you were standing there.'

'Oh dear God,' I moaned. 'It can't be. Impossible.'

'Anything is possible,' said Ewa Kaludis and started laughing again.

23

Verner Lindström hadn't got any younger.

'The statute of limitations will run out on the case in two months,' he explained as he adjusted his bow tie. 'But that's not why I want to talk to you. I'm writing a little memoir. I retired in the spring and you have to have something to keep yourself busy.'

We sat in the inner room at Linnaeus, a restaurant on Linnégatan. As far as I knew Lindström had taken the train down to Göteborg solely for this conversation; it was obvious that he had a hard time getting through the day as a pensioner.

It is what it is, I thought. Some people never learn to enjoy their rest; others seem born for it. After we'd eaten Lindström took out his Bronzol tube. I couldn't remember having seen those pastilles over the last ten to fifteen years, but maybe he had bought a lifetime supply in the early seventies.

'The fact of the matter is,' he said and put two pastilles in his mouth. 'The fact of the matter is that I don't have many unsolved cases to investigate. Just one murder. Bertil Albertsson.'

'That's how it can go,' I said. 'Well, you did your best.'

He chewed and rocked his head slowly from side to side like an old, tired bloodhound. 'The result,' he said. 'I don't give a toss about all the effort; it's the result that counts. Someone murdered that damned handball player on that damned clearing twenty-five years ago and in two months he'll get off scot-free.'

'Someone?' I said. 'I thought you'd decided it was my brother? You just weren't able to lock him up.'

Verner Lindström sighed.

'He or she,' he said. 'That was the thread we were following. I should tell you that we didn't spare her either. We spent a good part of that autumn interrogating her night and day, but she didn't crack. Damned fine woman. I wonder what happened to her.'

'No idea,' I said and shrugged. 'She probably moved overseas. She was the type.'

Lindström looked me over.

'I'm mostly interested in knowing if you might have any new information. Now that you don't have to protect your brother any more.'

'There are two months left,' I pointed out. 'You could still put him away.'

He smiled quickly and shook the Bronzol tube a few times, most likely to get an idea of how many were left.

'On my honour,' he then said and put it back in his inner pocket. 'You don't think that these old pensioner's hands want to dig anything up that's been buried for all these years?' He turned his palms up and looked at them and then at me with an expression of utter innocence. 'Anything,' he said. 'I'm interested in anything at all. It's not impossible that you held a thing or two back, you and your friend. You were only fourteen. It's not easy to know what to do in a situation like that.' He paused and hid his hands under the table, as if they weren't really living up to his expectations. 'And it's also possible that there was another person at Gennesaret that night.'

'Another person?' I asked. 'You mean Ewa Kaludis?'

He sighed again.

'No, the fact of the matter is that we never were sure if she was there or not. Even that is a mystery. She denied it. Henry denied it. It doesn't need to be more complicated than that. We could never prove that she was with him. But in any case there were indications that Henry had company.'

I thought for a few seconds. Mostly about the word 'indications'.

'Who might that have been?'

'That's what I was hoping you could tell me,' said Lindström.

'Haven't the foggiest,' I said. 'It would be better if you contacted Edmund. He was awake for a while that night.'

Lindström picked up a handkerchief and blew his nose.

'I've already spoken to him,' he explained somewhat impatiently. 'Twice.'

'Did he give you anything?'

'Hmm,' said Lindström. 'Priests are some of the worst to interrogate. Lucky that they're not often involved … Priests and pimps, I can't tell which I like less.'

'All right, then,' I said.

We sat in silence for a moment. Lindström had a college-ruled notebook lying next to his plate. He ceremoniously folded his handkerchief and looked at it, deep in thought. He didn't seem to be any happier for it, or more illumined. A sense of gloom spread across the table.

'Most unsolved murders have a number of factors in common,' he finally said and closed the pad.

'Really?' I said. 'What are they?'

'First and foremost: simplicity,' said Lindström. 'With Berra Albertsson … all the murderer needed to do was take two steps forward and then whack him with the hammer. Or the sledgehammer or whatever it was. One single blow, then it's done. Bury the murder weapon and forget about it ... Maybe hope for rain during the morning hours, and rain it did.'

He fell silent and speared a few stray peas with his fork. He took a long look at them—as if he'd suddenly realized that Berra Albertsson's murderer was hiding inside one.

Being a detective your whole life must make you a bit strange, I thought. Another half-minute passed.

'How could the murderer know that Albertsson was going to be there?' I asked. 'It seems odd. I've always wondered.'

'There's another possible scenario,' said Lindström. 'Berra Albertsson could have been hit by a person who was in the car with him. Someone who might have been in the back seat, for example.'

'Why?' I said. 'Who would that have been?'

'Good question,' said Lindström. 'Regardless of who hit him, the motive is problematic.'

'If it wasn't Henry?'

'Or Ewa Kaludis,' said Lindström.

I thought a while.

'How do you know that an unknown person was at Gennesaret that night?' I asked.

Lindström hesitated.

'An eye-witness account.'

'An eye-witness account? And whose was that?'

'I can't reveal that,' said Lindström and shrugged apologetically. 'I'm sorry.'

I stared at him, surprised.

'And the forensic evidence,' I asked. 'Clues and murder weapons and what not, how did that turn out?'

'Poorly,' said Lindström. 'On all accounts. The rain destroyed all the evidence at the crime scene. It wasn't even possible to see which of the cars had arrived first, your brother's or Berra's. Even if their positioning suggested that Henry had arrived earlier.'

'And the weapon?'

'It was never found,' Lindström stated. 'No, it is what it is. As long as no one comes forward, Bertil Albertsson's assailant will go free. In two months he'd be free in any case … but it would be a bonus to be able to write in my memoir that the case is solved. And I know who did it. That's why I'm here. Hmm.'

He paused again. Drank the last drop of wine and wiped his mouth. Collected himself before making his final plea.

'And you don't have anything that might shed some light on the story? Something you held back or that you remembered later?'

'No,' I said. 'I've thought about this for twenty-five years and I know as little today as I knew then. A madman who carried out the murder by chance, that's my suggestion. Have you explored that possibility thoroughly?'

Lindström didn't answer.

'Of course I would have come to the police if I'd known anything,' I added.

By now Lindström was starting to look resigned and I noticed that I didn't have much left of the respect that I had felt for him at the start of the sixties. I also understood that you're probably not a very good judge of character at fourteen, even though my brother had complimented me on it.

'I'm sorry,' I said. 'I'm very sorry, but it looks like this trip to Göteborg is going to be a waste of your time.'

'Don't say that,' said Lindström. 'The food wasn't bad and

I have another conversation scheduled.'

'Oh?' I said. 'With whom?'

He adjusted the Bronzol tube in his breast pocket and looked out of the window.

I never worked out if Verner Lindström really did have another subject to interview during his Göteborg trip, but two months later the Bertil Albertsson case was statute-barred. It was September 1987, and only afterward did Ewa and I discover that on the same night as the statute of limitations ran out we'd shared a lobster and a bottle of champagne.

As if we'd known about the date and deemed it worthy of celebration, somehow.

The real reason was that Karla had travelled up to her dad's in Eslöv and for once we had the flat on Palmstedtsgatan to ourselves.

24

Then the years passed and some things slipped into oblivion. Ewa Kaludis and I never had any children: for that time was too short. She was forty-seven when we met again and we both felt it was too risky. Her daughter Karla lived with us until about 1990, when she went off to study something or other in Paris, met a dark, wavy-haired Frenchman, and stayed. The frequency of my own children's visits increased at about the same rate as Ellinor's ire dissipated, and my eldest son Frans lived with us for a few months one autumn during his first term at the journalism college.

Even though Ewa's periods stopped a few months after she turned fifty, our love life didn't go through any corresponding changes. As far as I could tell, from discreet conversations I had with colleagues and others, we had an unusually robust sex life. No one ever guessed that there were ten years between us; I often have a hard time getting my head around it myself.

I suppose that's how it is. Some people aren't touched by the years, and on others you can count them double or triple.

The final chapter in the history of Gennesaret—or the Incident, as I liked to call it once upon a time—was written in the spring and summer of 1997.

One day in early May, from my ex-wife Ellinor, I found out that Father Wester up in Ånge had suffered a heart attack and was in hospital at Östersund. He was most likely on his death-bed, and because he still had Ellinor's phone number from the visit twelve years before, he'd called her and expressed a desire to speak to me.

I wasn't surprised that Edmund had had a heart attack; I thought about his enormous body and I decided to travel up to Östersund as soon as possible.

The opportunity arose a few days later, on Ascension Day, and I had four days of leave. I considered my travel options—plane, train or automobile—and settled on taking the car. I set off early on Thursday morning and about ten hours later I took my place in a tubular steel chair by Edmund's side.

He hadn't got any smaller since our last meeting; he lay beneath a yellow blanket like a stranded walrus and a considerable number of tubes were stuck into his arms and legs, pumping nourishment through his tremendous body. His face was a greyish purple like a mouldering plum, and it was hard to tell if he would survive or not.

Whatever the case, he seemed relieved to see me.

'So, tell me: how did things go with your father?' I said. 'Your real one. Did you ever look him up?'

Edmund gave a quick, strained smile.

'Yes, I looked him up,' he said. 'He was in a home outside Lycksele. Didn't recognize me. I don't think he remembered that he had a son—alcoholism and neglected diabetes. He died a few months after.'

I nodded. Of course it would end up that way. It was typical, somehow. Edmund was reluctant to talk about it; he had neither the desire nor the energy. There was a more pressing matter to attend to before it was too late.

A little over half an hour into our conversation, he grew too weak to continue. When we were done Edmund looked as peaceful as only the dead and severely ailing can. One of the last things he said was: 'It was still a brilliant summer, Erik. In spite of the Incident, it was a brilliant summer. I'll never forget it.'

'Neither will I,' I promised and patted him between two of the needles. 'Not for as long as I live.'

'Not for as long as I live,' Edmund repeated matter-of-factly.

And then he fell asleep. I stayed a while and watched him, and suddenly I was sure he was no longer in the hospital bed, but floating on his back in the lake at Gennesaret that balmy night after the pageantry of love in the window.

And I wished dearly for him to stay there.

I left with a sense of closure. Checked out of Hotel Zäta and headed south again. During the drive through the forests in Dalarna and Värmland, I decided to write down this entire story. Write it down and try to get it the right way around. If what I read somewhere is true, that every person has a book inside of them, then mine would be the story of the murder of Berra Albertsson.

But it wasn't mine alone.

I started on it as soon as we broke up for the summer holidays, and at the end of June—the week after Midsummer—I took a research trip back to the landscape of my childhood. Ewa vacillated about whether or not she should join me, but in the end she decided to stay at home; Karla had gleefully announced that she was thinking of coming for a visit with her Frenchman.

I hadn't set foot in the town on the plain since we moved away in the early sixties, and when the beautiful jasmine-scented summer night came rolling into my car as I drove along Stenevägen, I felt myself sinking into the well of time.

So much had changed and yet most of it was the same as ever. The exterior of the house on Idrottsgatan had been renovated, but the colours were the same and in our kitchen window facing the street were two pelargoniums, as before. I parked the car, walked out through the stretch of woodland and found the culvert in the ditch.

No one had touched it for thirty-five years. I had to crouch to fit, but never mind; I lit a cigarette, a Lucky Strike I'd bought at the railway station kiosk in Hallsberg. I shut my eyes and sat inside, smiling and close to tears.

What is a life? I thought. What the hell is a life?

I thought about Benny and Benny's mum; about Arse-Enok and Balthazar Lindblom and Edmund.

About my mother and father.

And Henry.

About the day a thousand years ago that Ewa Kaludis came riding into Stava School on her red Puch. Kim Novak.

And about my father's words: *It's going to be a difficult summer. Let's face it.*

My mother's listless hair and dying eyes in the hospital. What is a life?

The pattern of tiles in the loo. The tiny scars on Edmund's feet, proof that he'd once been in possession of twelve toes.

Ewa Kaludis. Her warm, strong hands on my shoulders and her naked body.

She's all I have left.

All I have managed to keep, I thought, is Ewa's beautiful body.

It could have been worse.

On the way out of town, I took Mossbanegatan south. Karlesson's shop was where it always had been, but the gum dispenser was no longer there. However, it had been extended as a corner cafe; the whole thing was called Gullan's Grill and I didn't feel like stopping.

The Kleva hill was as steep as before, even if it was less noticeable sitting in the car. I could still identify the place where Edmund had lain down and been sick after his valiant effort to conquer it in one go, and the way through the forest to Åsbro was the same down to every last bend. In the village itself they'd built a petrol station, but overall it was as I remembered it. I stopped outside Laxman's. I went in and bought a Ramlösa and an evening paper. The heavy-set woman at the till was in her fifties and had blooms of sweat under her arms, and there was nothing to contradict the notion that this was Britt Laxman.

A number of new summer houses had been built along Sjölyckevägen, but when I entered the forest I recalled every twist and dip of the winding gravel path. The Levis' house looked boarded up, but it had been like that then, too. I remembered the incantation as I drove past. Cancer-Treblinka-Love-Fuck-Death. I thought of Edmund's real dad who sat at the edge of his bed and cried for himself and for his abused boy, and then the memories began to flood in, and I didn't know I'd arrived at the parking area until I was standing on it.

The clearing seemed to have shrunk. Weeds and brushwood had encroached on its edges; maybe this was temporary but it seemed to be disused. I climbed out of the car and took in the start of both paths: the left down to the Lundins' was nearly overgrown; the right to Gennesaret looked trodden on and used. After a moment's hesitation I followed it down to the lake.

Gennesaret was where it had been, too. The same warped little hovel, but repainted and with a new roof. A garden shed out on the lawn and white garden furniture instead of our old rickety brown set. An outdoor grill and a TV antenna.

Nineties versus sixties. Forty-nine instead of fourteen.

Both the door and the kitchen window were open, so I knew that people were home. I didn't want to have to explain my errand, so I stayed on the path. Looked at everything through a lens thirty-five years thick; both the privy and the tumbledown shed were still there, and—above all—the floating dock. I was startled by my residual pride and before the tears started to fall, I turned on my heels and went back up the path to the parking spot.

I took the spade out of the boot of the car, walked straight across the road, measured between the trees and easily found the small, soft, moss-covered hollow.

I drove the spade into the earth and dug out a few shovels' worth. By the third shovel, I had hit the shaft. I wedged the blade under and soon I was standing there with the sledgehammer in my hands.

It was lighter than I remembered, but less ravaged by time than anything else I had seen that day. It was exactly as I remembered it. I gingerly brushed the shaft and the head clean. When the earth was gone, it could just as well have been lying with the rest of the tools in the shed all this time. Or it could even have been manufactured as recently as a few years ago.

If it weren't for a brownish-black, dried-up blotch on one end of the sledgehammer's head. It's incredible how some things endure. Sink their teeth in and endure.

I shunted the mounds of earth back into the hole and covered them with moss. Stuffed the sledgehammer in my black plastic bag. Tossed it into the footwell of the car on the passenger's side and drove away.

Two hours later I watched the bag sink to the bottom of a dark and muddy lake in the woods of Skara. The sun had started to set and the midges buzzed around my head, but I stood there a long while and tried to discern where the sledgehammer had broken through the water's surface. When there was no trace of it left, I shrugged and started the journey back to Göteborg.

A few days later Ewa and I lay awake one night after making love. We had the window propped wide open; it was one of those rare summer nights that only comes two or three times a year in Sweden. Music and laughter were spilling in from some sort of garden party at the neighbours'.

'That book you're writing?' Ewa asked and cautiously ran her hand over my stomach. 'How's it going?'

'Well enough,' I answered. 'It's coming along.'

She was silent for a while.

'I've always wondered something.'

'Oh?' I said. 'What?'

'Who actually killed Berra? You or Edmund? It had to be one of you.'

I turned around and buried my face between her breasts.

'Truer words were never spoken,' I said. 'It had to have been one of us.'

And then I told her who.

'What?' said Ewa. 'I can't hear what you're saying. Look at me.'

I breathed her scent in deeply and then that cloud unfurled inside me. It's remarkable how some clouds linger.

For more information, visit us at www.worldeditions.org